MORSE'S GREATEST MYSTERY
AND OTHER STORIES

Colin Dexter graduated from Cambridge in 1953. He spent his years wholly in education until his retirement in 1988, first teaching Greek and Latin, then moving to Oxford in 1966 to work for the University Examination Board.

His first Inspector Morse novel, *Last Bus to Woodstock*, was published in 1975, and in addition to winning the Crime Writers Association Gold Dagger Award twice – for *The Way Through the Woods* and *The Wench is Dead* – Colin Dexter has also been awarded Silver Daggers by the CWA for *Service of all the Dead* and *The Dead of Jericho*. The most recent novel, *Death is Now my Neighbour*, became a number one bestseller on hardback publication in 1996.

The Inspector Morse novels have been adapted for the small screen, with huge success, in Central Television's series starring John Thaw and Kevin Whately. In 1993 Colin Dexter achieved a long-held ambition – a speaking part (two words) in the seventh *Inspector Morse* TV series.

MORSE'S
GREATEST MYSTERY
AND OTHER STORIES

COLIN DEXTER

PAN BOOKS

First published 1993 by Macmillan London

This special edition published 1998 by Pan Books
an imprint of Macmillan Publishers Limited
25 Eccleston Place London SW1W 9NF
and Basingstoke

Associated companies throughout the world

ISBN 0 330 37642X

'Morse's Greatest Mystery' © 1987. 'Evans Tries an O-Level' © 1977; this story
first appeared in *Winter's Crimes 7* (Macmillan, 1976). 'Dead as a Dodo' © 1991. 'At
the Lulu-Bar Motel' © 1981; this story first appeared in *Winter's Crimes 13*
(Macmillan, 1981). 'Neighbourhood Watch' © 1992. 'A Case of Mis-Identity' ©
1989; this story first appeared in *Winter's Crimes 21* (Macmillan London, 1989).

The author and publishers wish to thank the following for the use of copyright
materials: the extract from *The Oxford Companion to English Literature* edited by
Margaret Drabble (5th edition, 1985) by permission of the Oxford University Press,
and the extract from 'Monologue of a Blue Fox on an Alaskan Animal Farm' by
Yevtushenko by permission of the *New York Times*.

1 3 5 7 9 8 6 4 2

A CIP catalogue record for this book is available
from the British Library.

Printed and bound in Great Britain by
Mackays of Chatham PLC, Chatham, Kent

CONTENTS

MORSE'S
GREATEST MYSTERY

> 'Hallo!' growled Scrooge, in his accustomed voice as near
> as he could feign it. 'What do you mean by coming here at
> this time of day?'
>
> (Dickens, *A Christmas Carol*)

He had knocked diffidently at Morse's North Oxford flat.
Few had been invited into those book-lined, Wagner-haunted
rooms: and even he – Sergeant Lewis – had never felt himself
an over-welcome guest. Even at Christmas time. Not that it
sounded much like the season of good-will as Morse waved
Lewis inside and concluded his ill-tempered conversation
with the bank manager.

'Look! If I keep a couple of hundred in my current account,
that's *my* look-out. I'm not even asking for any interest on it.
All I *am* asking is that you don't stick these bloody bank
charges on when I go – what? once, twice a year? – into the
red. It's not that I'm mean with money' – Lewis's eyebrows
ascended a centimetre – 'but if you charge me again I want
you to ring and tell me *why*!'

Morse banged down the receiver and sat silent.

'You don't sound as if you've caught much of the
Christmas spirit,' ventured Lewis.

'I don't like Christmas – never have.'

'You staying in Oxford, sir?'

'I'm going to decorate.'

'What – decorate the Christmas cake?'

'Decorate the kitchen. I don't like Christmas cake – never
did.'

'You sound more like Scrooge every minute, sir.'

'*And* I shall read a Dickens novel. I always do over Christmas. *Re*-read, rather.'

'If I were just *starting* on Dickens, which one—?'

'I'd put *Bleak House* first, *Little Dorrit* second—'

The phone rang and Morse's secretary at HQ informed him that he'd won a £50 gift-token in the Police Charity Raffle, and this time Morse cradled the receiver with considerably better grace.

'"Scrooge", did you say, Lewis? I'll have you know I bought five tickets – a quid apiece! – in that Charity Raffle.'

'I bought five tickets myself, sir.'

Morse smiled complacently. 'Let's be more charitable, Lewis! It's *supporting* these causes that's important, not *winning*.'

'I'll be in the car, sir,' said Lewis quietly. In truth, he was beginning to feel irritated. Morse's irascibility he could stomach; but he couldn't stick hearing much more about Morse's selfless generosity!

Morse's old Jaguar was in dock again ('Too mean to buy a new one!' his colleagues claimed) and it was Lewis's job that day to ferry the chief inspector around; doubtless, too (if things went to form) to treat him to the odd pint or two. Which indeed appeared a fair probability, since Morse had so managed things on that Tuesday morning that their arrival at the George would coincide with opening time. As they drove out past the railway station, Lewis told Morse what he'd managed to discover about the previous day's events . . .

The patrons of the George had amassed £400 in aid of the Littlemore Charity for Mentally Handicapped Children, and this splendid total was to be presented to the Charity's Secretary at the end of the week, with a photographer

4

promised from *The Oxford Times* to record the grand occasion. Mrs Michaels, the landlady, had been dropped off at the bank in Carfax by her husband at about 10.30 a.m., and had there exchanged a motley assemblage of coins and notes for forty brand-new tenners. After this she had bought several items (including grapes for a daughter just admitted to hospital) before catching a minibus back home, where she had arrived just after midday. The money, in a long white envelope, was in her shopping bag, together with her morning's purchases. Her husband had not yet returned from the Cash and Carry Stores, and on re-entering the George via the saloon bar, Mrs Michaels had heard the telephone ringing. Thinking that it was probably the hospital (it was) she had dumped her bag on the bar counter and rushed to answer it. On her return, the envelope was gone.

At the time of the theft, there had been about thirty people in the saloon bar, including the regular OAPs, the usual cohort of pool-playing unemployables, and a pre-Christmas party from a local firm. And – yes! – from the very beginning Lewis had known that the chances of recovering the money were virtually nil. Even so, the three perfunctory interviews that Morse conducted appeared to Lewis to be sadly unsatisfactory.

After listening a while to the landlord's unilluminating testimony, Morse asked him why it had taken him so long to conduct his business at the Cash and Carry; and although the explanation given seemed perfectly adequate, Morse's dismissal of this first witness had seemed almost offensively abrupt. And no man could have been more quickly or more effectively antagonized than the temporary barman (on duty the previous morning) who refused to answer Morse's

5

brusque enquiry about the present state of his overdraft. What then of the attractive, auburn-haired Mrs Michaels? After a rather lop-sided smile had introduced Morse to her regular if slightly nicotine-stained teeth, that distressed lady had been unable to fight back her tears as she sought to explain to Morse why she'd insisted on some genuine notes for the publicity photographer instead of a phonily magnified cheque.

But wait! Something dramatic had just happened to Morse, Lewis could see that: as if the light had suddenly shined upon a man that hitherto had sat in darkness. He (Morse) now asked – amazingly! – whether by any chance the good lady possessed a pair of bright green, high-heeled leather shoes; and when she replied that, yes, she did, Morse smiled serenely, as though he had solved the secret of the universe, and promptly summoned into the lounge bar not only the three he'd just interviewed but all those now in the George who had been drinking there the previous morning.

As they waited, Morse asked for the serial numbers of the stolen notes, and Lewis passed over a scrap of paper on which some figures had been hastily scribbled in blotchy Biro. 'For Christ's sake, man!' hissed Morse. 'Didn't they teach you to write at school?'

Lewis breathed heavily, counted to five, and then painstakingly rewrote the numbers on a virginal piece of paper: 773741–773780. At which numbers Morse glanced cursorily before sticking the paper in his pocket, and proceeding to address the George's regulars.

He was *virtually* certain (he said) of who had stolen the money. What he was *absolutely* sure about was exactly where that money was *at that very moment*. He had the serial numbers of the notes – but that was of no importance whatsoever now. The thief might well have been tempted to spend the money earlier – but not any more! And why not? Because at this Christmas time that person *no longer had the power to resist his better self*.

In that bar, stilled now and silent as the grave itself, the faces of Morse's audience seemed mesmerized – and remained so as Morse gave his instructions that the notes should be replaced in their original envelope and returned (he cared not by what means) to Sergeant Lewis's office at Thames Valley Police HQ *within the next twenty-four hours*.

As they drove back, Lewis could restrain his curiosity no longer. 'You really *are* confident that—?'

'Of course!'

'I never seem to be able to put the clues together myself, sir.'

'Clues? What clues, Lewis? I didn't know we had any.'

'Well, those shoes, for example. How do they fit in?'

'Who said they fitted in anywhere? It's just that I used to know an auburn-haired beauty who had six – *six*, Lewis! – pairs of bright green shoes. They suited her, she said.'

'So . . . they've got nothing to do with the case at all?'

'Not so far as I know,' muttered Morse.

The next morning a white envelope was delivered to Lewis's office, though no one at reception could recall when or whence it had arrived. Lewis immediately rang Morse to congratulate him on the happy outcome of the case.

'There's just one thing, sir. I'd kept that scrappy bit of paper with the serial numbers on it, and these are brand-new notes all right – but they're not the same ones!'

'Really?' Morse sounded supremely unconcerned.

'You're not worried about it?'

'Good Lord, no! You just get that money back to ginger-knob at the George, and tell her to settle for a jumbo-cheque next time! Oh, and one other thing, Lewis. I'm on *leave*. So no interruptions from anybody – understand?'

'Yes, sir. And, er . . . Happy Christmas, sir!'

'And to you, old friend!' replied Morse quietly.

The bank manager rang just before lunch that same day. 'It's about the four hundred pounds you withdrew yesterday, Inspector. I did promise to ring about any further bank charges—'

'I explained to the girl,' protested Morse. 'I needed the money quickly.'

'Oh, it's perfectly all right. But you did say you'd call in this morning to transfer—'

'Tomorrow! I'm up a ladder with a paint brush at the moment.'

Morse put down the receiver and again sank back in the armchair with the crossword. But his mind was far away, and some of the words he himself had spoken kept echoing around his brain: something about one's better self . . . And he smiled, for he knew that this would be a Christmas he might enjoy almost as much as the children up at Littlemore, perhaps. He had solved so many mysteries in his life. Was he now, he wondered, beginning to glimpse the solution to the greatest mystery of them all?

EVANS TRIES
AN O-LEVEL

Dramatis Personae

The Secretary of the Examinations Board

The Governor of HM Prison, Oxford

James Evans, a prisoner

Mr Jackson, a prison officer

Mr Stephens, a prison officer

The Reverend S. McLeery, an invigilator

Detective Superintendent Carter

Detective Chief Inspector Bell

The unexamined life is not worth living.

(Plato)

It was in early March when the Secretary of the Examinations Board received the call from Oxford Prison.

'It's a slightly unusual request, Governor, but I don't see why we shouldn't try to help. Just the one fellow, you say?'

'That's it. Chap called Evans. Started night classes in O-level German last September. Says he's dead keen to get some sort of academic qualification.'

'Is he any good?'

'He was the only one in the class, so you can say he's had individual tuition all the time, really. Would have cost him a packet if he'd been outside.'

'We-ell, let's give him a chance, shall we?'

'That's jolly kind of you. What exactly's the procedure now?'

'Oh, don't worry about that. I'll be sending you all the forms and stuff. What's his name, you say? Evans?'

'James Roderick Evans.' It sounded rather grand.

'Just one thing, Governor. He's not a violent sort of fellow, is he? I don't want to know his criminal record or anything like that, but—'

'No. There's no record of violence. Quite a pleasant sort of chap, they tell me. Bit of a card, really. One of the stars at the Christmas concert. Imitations, you know the sort of thing: Mike Yarwood stuff. No, he's just a congenital kleptomaniac, that's all.' The Governor was tempted to add something else,

11

but he thought better of it. He'd look after *that* particular side of things himself.

'Presumably,' said the Secretary, 'you can arrange a room where—'

'No problem. He's in a cell on his own. If you've no objections, he can sit the exam in there.'

'That's fine.'

'And we could easily get one of the parsons from St Mary Mags to invigilate, if that's—'

'Fine, yes. They seem to have a helluva lot of parsons there, don't they?' The two men chuckled good-naturedly, and the Secretary had a final thought. 'At least there's one thing. You shouldn't have much trouble keeping him *incommunicado*, should you?'

The Governor chuckled politely once more, reiterated his thanks, and slowly cradled the phone.

Evans!

'Evans the Break' as the prison officers called him. Three times he'd escaped from prison, and but for the recent wave of unrest in the maximum-security establishments up north, he wouldn't now be gracing the Governor's premises in Oxford; and the Governor was going to make absolutely certain that he wouldn't be *dis*gracing them. Not that Evans was a *real* burden: just a persistent, nagging presence. He'd be all right in Oxford, though: the Governor would see to that – would see to it personally. And besides, there was just a possibility that Evans was genuinely interested in O-level German. Just a slight possibility. Just a very slight possibility.

*

At 8.30 p.m. on Monday 7 June, Evans's German teacher shook him by the hand in the heavily guarded Recreational Block, just across from D Wing.

'*Guten Glück*, Herr Evans.'

'Pardon?'

'I said, "Good luck". Good luck for tomorrow.'

'Oh. Thanks, er, I mean, er, *Danke schön*.'

'You haven't a cat in hell's chance of getting through, of course, but—'

'I may surprise everybody,' said Evans.

At 8.30 the following morning, Evans had a visitor. Two visitors, in fact. He tucked his grubby string-vest into his equally grubby trousers, and stood up from his bunk, smiling cheerfully. 'Mornin', Mr Jackson. This is indeed an honour.'

Jackson was the senior prison officer on D Wing, and he and Evans had already become warm enemies. At Jackson's side stood Officer Stephens, a burly, surly-looking man, only recently recruited to the profession.

Jackson nodded curtly. 'And how's our little Einstein this morning, then?'

'Wasn't 'e a mathematician, Mr Jackson?'

'He was a bloody Kraut,' snapped Jackson. Evans's quiet voice always riled him, and Evans's present insight into his own vast ignorance riled him even more.

'I think 'e was a Jew, Mr Jackson.'

'I don't give a monkey's fuck what he was, you scruffy sod.'

'Scruffy' was, perhaps, the right word. Evans's face was

13

unshaven, and he wore a filthy-looking red-and-white bobble hat upon his head. 'Give me a *chance*, Mr Jackson. I was just goin' to shave when you bust in.'

'Which reminds me.' Jackson turned his eyes on Stephens. 'Make sure you take his razor out of the cell when he's finished scraping that ugly mug of his. Clear? One of these days he'll do us all a favour and cut his bloody throat.'

For a few seconds Evans looked thoughtfully at the man standing ramrod straight in front of him, a string of Second World War medals proudly paraded over his left breast-pocket. 'Mr Jackson? Was it *you* who took me nail-scissors away?' Evans had always worried about his hands.

'*And* your nail-file, you poncy twit.'

'Look!' For a moment Evans's eyes smouldered danger-ously, but Jackson was ready for him.

'Orders of the Governor, Evans.' He leaned forward and leered, his voice dropping to a harsh, contemptuous whisper. 'You want to *complain*?'

Evans shrugged his shoulders lightly. The crisis was over.

'You've got half an hour to smarten yourself up, Evans – and take that bloody hat off!'

'Me 'at? Huh!' Evans put his right hand lovingly on top of the filthy woollen, and smiled sadly. 'D'you know, Mr Jackson, it's the only thing that's ever brought me any sort o' luck in life. Kind o' lucky charm, if you know what I mean. And today I thought – well, with me exam and all that . . .'

Buried somewhere in Jackson, beneath all the bluster and the bullshit, was a tiny core of compassion; and Evans knew it.

'Just this once, then, Shirley Temple.' (If there was one

thing that Jackson genuinely loathed about Evans it was his long, wavy hair.) 'And get bloody shaving!'

At 8.45 the same morning the Reverend Stuart McLeery left his bachelor flat in Broad Street and stepped out briskly towards Carfax. The weatherman reported temperatures considerably below the normal for early June, and a long black overcoat and a shallow-crowned clerical hat provided welcome protection from the steady drizzle which had set in half an hour earlier and which now spattered the thick lenses of his spectacles. In his right hand he was carrying a small brown suitcase, which contained all that he would need for his morning duties, including a sealed question-paper envelope, a yellow invigilation form, a special 'authentication' card from the Examinations Board, a paper-knife, a Bible (he was to speak to the Women's Guild that afternoon on the book of Ruth), and a current copy of *The Church Times*.

The two-hour examination was scheduled to start at 9.15 a.m.

Evans was lathering his face vigorously when Stephens brought in two small square tables, and set them opposite each other in the narrow space between the bunk on the one side and on the other the distempered stone wall, plastered at eye-level with a proud row of naked women, vast-breasted and voluptuous. Next, Stephens brought in two hard chairs, the slightly less battered of which he placed in front of the table which stood nearer the cell door.

Jackson put in a brief final appearance. 'Behave yourself, laddy!'

Evans turned and nodded.

'And these' – (Jackson pointed to the pin-ups) – 'off!'

Evans turned and nodded again. 'I was goin' to take 'em down anyway. A minister, isn't 'e? The chap comin' to sit in, I mean.'

'And how did you know that?' asked Jackson quietly.

'Well, I 'ad to sign some forms, didn't I? And I couldn't 'elp—'

'You sneaky little bastard.'

Evans drew the razor carefully down his left cheek, and left a neat swath in the white lather. 'Can I ask you something, Mr Jackson? Why did they 'ave to bug me bloody cell?' He nodded his head vaguely to a point above the door.

'Not a very neat job,' conceded Jackson.

'They're not – they don't honestly think I'm goin' to try to—'

'They're taking no chances, Evans. Nobody in his bloody senses would take any chances with *you*.'

'Who's goin' to listen in?'

'I'll tell you who's going to listen in, laddy. It's the Governor himself, see? He don't trust you a bloody inch – and nor do I. I'll be watching you like a bleedin' hawk, Evans, so keep your nose clean. Clear?' He walked towards the door. 'And while we're on the subject of your nose, Evans, it's about time you changed that filthy snot-rag dangling from your arse pocket. Clear?'

Evans nodded. He'd already thought of that, and Number Two Handkerchief was lying ready on the bunk – a neatly folded square of off-white linen.

'Just one more thing, Einstein.'

'Ya? Wha's 'at?'

'Good luck, old son.'

In the little lodge just inside the prison's main gates, the Reverend S. McLeery signed his name neatly in the visitors' book, and thence walked side by side with a silent prison officer across the exercise yard to D Wing, where he was greeted by Jackson. The Wing's heavy outer door was unlocked, and locked behind them, the heavy inner door the same, and McLeery was handed into Stephens's keeping.

'Get the razor?' murmured Jackson.

Stephens nodded.

'Well, keep your eyes skinned. Clear?'

Stephens nodded again; and McLeery, his feet clanging up the iron stairs, followed his new guide, and finally stood before a cell door, where Stephens opened the peep-hole and looked through.

'That's him, sir.'

Evans, facing the door, sat quietly at the farther of the two tables, his whole attention riveted to a textbook of elementary German grammar. Stephens took the key from its ring, and the cell lock sprang back with a thudded, metallic twang.

It was 9.10 a.m. when the Governor switched on the receiver. He had instructed Jackson to tell Evans of the temporary little precaution – that was only fair. (As if Evans wouldn't spot it!) But wasn't it all a bit theatrical? Schoolboyish, almost? How on earth was Evans going to try anything on today? If he was so anxious to make another break, why in

17

heaven's name hadn't he tried it from the Recreational Block? Much easier. But he hadn't. And there he was now – sitting in a locked cell, all the prison officers on the alert, two more locked doors between his cell and the yard, and a yard with a wall as high as a haystack. Yes, Evans was as safe as houses . . .

Anyway, it wouldn't be any trouble at all to have the receiver turned on for the next couple of hours or so. It wasn't as if there was going to be anything to listen to, was it? Amongst other things, an invigilator's duty was to ensure that the strictest silence was observed. But . . . but still that little nagging doubt! Might Evans try to take advantage of McLeery? Get him to smuggle in a chisel or two, or a rope-ladder, or—

The Governor sat up sharply. It was all very well getting rid of any potential weapon that *Evans* could have used; but what about *McLeery*? What if, quite unwittingly, the innocent McLeery had brought in something himself? A jack-knife, perhaps? And what if Evans held him hostage with such a weapon? Sort of hi-jack-knifed him?

The Governor reached for the phone. It was 9.12 a.m.

The examinee and the invigilator had already been introduced by Stephens when Jackson came back and shouted to McLeery through the cell door. 'Can you come outside a minute, sir? You too, Stephens.'

Jackson quickly explained the Governor's worries, and McLeery patiently held out his arms at shoulder level whilst Jackson lightly frisked his clothes. 'Something hard here, sir.'

18

'Ma reading glasses,' replied McLeery, looking down at the spectacle case.

Jackson quickly reassured him, and bending down on the landing thumb-flicked the catches on the suitcase. He picked up each envelope in turn, carefully passed his palms along their surfaces – and seemed satisfied. He riffled cursorily through a few pages of Holy Writ, and vaguely shook *The Church Times*. All right, so far. But one of the objects in McLeery's suitcase was puzzling him sorely.

'Do you mind telling me why you've brought this, sir?' He held up a smallish semi-inflated rubber ring, such as a young child with a waist of about twelve inches might have struggled into. 'You thinking of going for a swim, sir?'

McLeery's hitherto amiable demeanour was slightly ruffled by this tasteless little pleasantry, and he answered Jackson somewhat sourly. 'If ye must know, I suffer from haemorrhoids, and when I'm sitting down for any length o' time—'

'Very sorry, sir. I didn't mean to, er . . .' The embarrassment was still reddening Jackson's cheeks when he found the paper-knife at the bottom of the case. 'I think I'd better keep this though, if you don't mind, that is, sir.'

It was 9.18 a.m. before the Governor heard their voices again, and it was clear that the examination was going to be more than a little late in getting under way.

McLeery: 'Ye've got a watch?'
Evans: 'Yes, sir.'
McLeery: 'I'll be telling ye when to start, and again when ye've five minutes left. A' right?'

Silence.

McLeery: 'There's plenty more o' this writing paper should ye need it.'

Silence.

McLeery: 'Now. Write the name of the paper, 021–1, in the top left-hand corner.'

Silence.

McLeery: 'In the top right-hand corner write your index number – 313. And in the box just below that, write your centre number – 271. A' right?'

Silence. 9.20 a.m.

McLeery: 'I'm now going to—'

Evans: "E's not goin' to stay 'ere, is 'e?'

McLeery: 'I don't know about that. I—'

Stephens: 'Mr Jackson's given me strict instructions to—'

Evans: "Ow the 'ell am I supposed to concentrate on me exam with a bleedin' screw breathin' down me neck? Christ! Sorry, sir, I didn't mean—'

The Governor reached for the phone. 'Jackson? Ah, good. Get Stephens out of that cell, will you? I think we're perhaps overdoing things.'

'As you wish, sir.'

The Governor heard the exchanges in the cell, heard the door clang to once more, and heard McLeery announce that the examination had begun at last.

It was 9.25 a.m.; and there was a great calm.

At 9.40 a.m. the Examinations Board rang through, and the Assistant Secretary with special responsibility for modern languages asked to speak to the Governor. The examination had already started, no doubt? Ah, a quarter of an hour ago. Yes. Well, there was a correction slip which some fool had forgotten to place in the examination package. Very brief. Could the Governor please . . . ?

'Yes, of course. I'll put you straight through to Mr Jackson in D Wing. Hold the line a minute.'

Was this the sort of thing the Governor had feared? Was the phone call a fake? Some signal? Some secret message . . .? But he could check on that immediately. He dialled the number of the Examinations Board, but heard only the staccato bleeps of a line engaged. But then the line *was* engaged, wasn't it? Yes. Not very intelligent, that . . .

Two minutes later he heard some whispered communications in the cell, and then McLeery's broad Scots voice:

'Will ye please stop writing a wee while, Mr Evans, and listen carefully. Candidates offering German, 021-1, should note the following correction. "On page three, line fifteen, the fourth word should read *goldenen*, not *goldene*; and the whole phrase will therefore read *zum goldenen Löwen*, not *zum goldene Löwen*." I will repeat that . . .'

The Governor listened and smiled. He had taken German in the sixth form himself, and he remembered all about the agreements of adjectives. And so did McLeery, by the sound of things, for the minister's pronunciation was most impressive. But what about Evans? *He* probably didn't know what an adjective *was*.

The phone rang again. The Magistrates' Court. They needed a prison van and a couple of prison officers. Remand case. And within two minutes the Governor was wondering

21

whether *that* could be a hoax. He told himself not to be so silly. His imagination was beginning to run riot.

Evans!

For the first quarter of an hour Stephens had dutifully peered through the peep-hole at intervals of one minute or so; and after that, every two minutes. At 10.45 a.m. he nipped off to the gents', and was in such a hurry to get back that he found he'd dribbled down his trousers. But everything was still all right as he looked through the peep-hole once more. It took four or five seconds – no more. What was the point? It was always more or less the same. Evans, his pen between his lips, sat staring straight in front of him towards the door, seeking – it seemed – some sorely needed inspiration from somewhere. And opposite him McLeery, seated slightly askew from the table now: his face in semi-profile; his hair (as Stephens had noticed earlier) amateurishly clipped pretty closely to the scalp; his eyes behind the pebble lenses peering short-sightedly at *The Church Times*; his right index finger hooked beneath the narrow clerical collar; and the fingers of the left hand, the nails meticulously manicured, slowly stroking the short black beard.

At 10.50 a.m. the receiver crackled to life and the Governor realized he'd almost forgotten Evans for a few minutes.

Evans: 'Please, sir!' (A whisper)

Evans: 'Please, sir!' (Louder)

Evans: 'Would you mind if I put a blanket round me shoulders, sir? It's a bit parky in 'ere, isn't it?'

	Silence.
Evans:	'There's one on me bunk 'ere, sir.'
McLeery:	'Be quick about it.'
	Silence.

At 10.51 a.m. Stephens was more than a little surprised to see a grey regulation blanket draped round Evans's shoulders, and he frowned slightly and looked at the examinee more closely. But Evans, the pen still between his teeth, was staring just as vacantly as before. Blankly beneath a blanket ... Should Stephens report the slight irregularity? Anything at all fishy, hadn't Jackson said? Mm. He looked through the peep-hole once again, and even as he did so Evans pulled the dirty blanket more closely to himself. Was he planning a sudden batman leap to suffocate McLeery in the blanket? Don't be daft! There was never any sun on this side of the prison; no heating, either, during the summer months, and it could get quite chilly in some of the cells. Mm. Stephens decided to revert to his earlier every-minute observation.

At 11.20 a.m. the receiver once more crackled across the silence of the Governor's office, and McLeery informed Evans that only five minutes remained. The examination was almost over now, but something still gnawed away quietly in the Governor's mind. He reached for the phone once more.

At 11.22 a.m. Jackson shouted along the corridor to Stephens. The Governor wanted to speak with him – '*Hurry, man!*' Stephens picked up the phone apprehensively and listened to the rapidly spoken orders. Stephens himself was to accompany McLeery to the main prison gates. Understood? Stephens personally was to make absolutely sure that the door was locked on Evans after McLeery had left the cell. Understood?

Understood.

At 11.25 a.m. the Governor heard the final exchanges.

McLeery: 'Stop writing, please.'
            Silence.
McLeery: 'Put your sheets in order and see they're correctly
             numbered.'
            Silence.
            Scraping of chairs and tables.
Evans: 'Thank you very much, sir.'
McLeery: 'A' right, was it?'
Evans: 'Not too bad.'
McLeery: 'Good . . . Mr Stephens!' (Very loud)

The Governor heard the door clang to for the last time. The examination was over.

'How did he get on, do you think?' asked Stephens as he walked beside McLeery to the main gates.

'Och. I canna think he's distinguished hissel, I'm afraid.' His Scots accent seemed broader than ever, and his long black overcoat, reaching almost to his knees, fostered the illusion that he had suddenly grown slimmer.

Stephens felt pleased that the Governor had asked *him*, and not Jackson, to see McLeery off the premises, and all in all

24

the morning had gone pretty well. But something stopped him from making his way directly to the canteen for a belated cup of coffee. He wanted to take just one last look at Evans. It was like a programme he'd seen on TV – about a woman who could never *really* convince herself that she'd locked the front door when she'd gone to bed: often she'd got up twelve, fifteen, sometimes twenty times to check the bolts.

He re-entered D Wing, made his way along to Evans's cell, and opened the peep-hole once more. *Oh, no!* CHRIST, NO! There, sprawled back in Evans's chair was a man (for a semi-second Stephens thought it must be Evans), a grey regulation blanket slipping from his shoulders, the front of his closely cropped, irregularly tufted hair awash with fierce red blood which had dripped already through the small black beard, and was even now spreading horribly over the white clerical collar and down into the black clerical front.

Stephens shouted wildly for Jackson: and the words appeared to penetrate the curtain of blood that veiled McLeery's ears, for the minister's hand felt feebly for a handkerchief from his pocket, and held it to his bleeding head, the blood seeping slowly through the white linen. He gave a long low moan, and tried to speak. But his voice trailed away, and by the time Jackson had arrived and despatched Stephens to ring the police and the ambulance, the handkerchief was a sticky, squelchy wodge of cloth.

McLeery slowly raised himself, his face twisted tightly with pain. 'Dinna worry about the ambulance, man! I'm a' right ... I'm a' right ... Get the police! I know ... I know where ... he ...' He closed his eyes and another drip of blood splashed like a huge red raindrop on the wooden floor. His hand felt along the table, found the German question paper, and grasped it tightly in his bloodstained hand. 'Get the Governor! I know . . . I know where Evans . . .'

Almost immediately sirens were sounding, prison officers barked orders, puzzled prisoners pushed their way along the corridors, doors were banged and bolted, and phones were ringing everywhere. And within a minute McLeery, with Jackson and Stephens supporting him on either side, his face now streaked and caked with drying blood, was greeted in the prison yard by the Governor, perplexed and grim.

'We must get you to hospital immediately. I just don't—'

'Ye've called the police?'

'Yes, yes. They're on their way. But—'

'I'm a' right. I'm a' right. Look! Look here!' Awkwardly he opened the German question paper and thrust it before the Governor's face. 'It's there! D'ye see what I *mean*?'

The Governor looked down and realized what McLeery was trying to tell him. A photocopied sheet had been carefully and cleverly superimposed over the last (originally blank) page of the question paper.

'Ye see what they've done, Governor. Ye see . . .' His voice trailed off again, as the Governor, dredging the layers of long-neglected learning, willed himself to translate the German text before him:

Sie sollen dem schon verabredeten Plan genau folgen. Der wichtige Zeitpunkt ist drei Minuten vor Ende des Examens . . . 'You must follow the plan already somethinged. The vital point in time is three minutes before the end of the examination but something something – something something . . . Don't hit

26

him too hard – remember, he's a minister! And don't overdo the Scots accent when . . .'

A fast-approaching siren wailed to its crescendo, the great doors of the prison yard were pushed back, and a white police car squealed to a jerky halt beside them.

Detective Superintendent Carter swung himself out of the passenger seat and saluted the Governor. 'What the hell's happening, sir?' And, turning to McLeery: 'Christ! Who's hit *him*?'

But McLeery cut across whatever explanation the Governor might have given. 'Elsfield Way, officer! I know where Evans . . .' He was breathing heavily, and leaned for support against the side of the car, where the imprint of his hand was left in tarnished crimson.

In bewilderment Carter looked to the Governor for guidance. 'What—?'

'Take him with you, if you think he'll be all right. He's the only one who seems to know what's happening.'

Carter opened the back door and helped McLeery inside; and within a few seconds the car leaped away in a spurt of gravel.

'Elsfield Way', McLeery had said; and there it was staring up at the Governor from the last few lines of the German text: 'From Elsfield Way drive to the Headington roundabout, where . . .' Yes, of course. *The Examinations Board was in Elsfield Way*, and someone from the Board must have been involved in the escape plan from the very beginning: the question paper itself, the correction slip . . .

The Governor turned to Jackson and Stephens. 'I don't need to tell you what's happened, do I?' His voice sounded almost calm in its scathing contempt. 'And which one of you two morons was it who took Evans for a nice little walk to the main gates and waved him bye-bye?'

'It was me, sir,' stammered Stephens. 'Just like you told me, sir. I could have sworn—'

'What? Just like I told you, you say? What the hell—?'

'When you rang, sir, and told me to—'

'When was that?' The Governor's voice was a whiplash now.

'You know, sir. About twenty past eleven, just before—'

'You blithering idiot, man! It wasn't *me* who rang you. Don't you realize—' But what was the use? He *had* used the telephone at that time, but only to try (unsuccessfully, once more) to get through to the Examinations Board.

He shook his head in growing despair and turned on the senior prison officer. 'As for you, Jackson! How long have you been pretending you've got a brain, eh? Well, I'll tell you something, Jackson. Your skull's *empty*. Absolutely bloody empty!' It was Jackson who had spent two hours in Evans's cell the previous evening; and it was Jackson who had confidently reported that there was nothing hidden away there – nothing at all. And yet Evans had somehow managed to conceal not only a false beard, a pair of spectacles, a dog-collar and all the rest of his clerical paraphernalia, but also some sort of weapon with which he'd given McLeery such a terrible blow across the head. Aurrgh!

A prison van backed alongside, but the Governor made no immediate move. He looked down again at the last line of the German: '. . . to the Headington roundabout, where

28

you go straight over and make your way to ... to Neugraben.' 'Neugraben'? Where on earth—? 'New' something. 'Newgrave'? Never heard of it. There was a 'Wargrave', somewhere near Reading, but ... No, it was probably a code word, or— And then it hit him. Newbury! God, yes! Newbury was a pretty big sort of place but—

He rapped out his orders to the driver. 'St Aldates Police Station, and step on it! Take Jackson and Stephens here, and when you get there ask for Bell. Chief Inspector Bell. Got that?'

He leaped the stairs to his office three at a time, got Bell on the phone immediately, and put the facts before him.

'We'll get him, sir,' said Bell. 'We'll get him, with a bit o' luck.'

The Governor sat back, and lit a cigarette. Ye gods! What a beautifully laid plan it had all been! What a clever sod Evans was! Careless leaving that question paper behind; but then, they all made their mistakes somewhere along the line. Well, *almost* all of them. That's why they were doing their porridge, and that's why very very shortly Mr clever-clever Evans would be back inside doing *his* once more.

The phone on his desk erupted in a strident burst, and Superintendent Carter informed him that McLeery had spotted Evans driving off along Elsfield Way; they'd got the number of the car all right and had given chase immediately, but had lost him at the Headington roundabout; he must have doubled back into the city.

'No,' said the Governor quietly. 'No, he's on his way to Newbury.' He explained his reasons for believing so, and left it at that. It was a police job now – not his. He was just another good-for-a-giggle, gullible governor, that was all.

'By the way, Carter. I hope you managed to get McLeery to hospital all right?'

'Yes. He's in the Radcliffe now. Really groggy, he was, when we got to the Examination offices, and they rang for the ambulance from there.'

The Governor rang the Radcliffe a few minutes later and asked for the accident department.

'McLeery, you say?'

'Yes. He's a parson.'

'I don't think there's anyone—'

'Yes, there is. You'll find one of your ambulances picked him up from Elsfield Way about—'

'Oh, *that*. Yes, we sent an ambulance all right, but when we got there, the fellow had gone. No one seemed to know where he was. Just vanished! Not a sign—'

But the Governor was no longer listening, and the truth seemed to hit him with an almost physical impact somewhere in the back of his neck.

A quarter of an hour later they found the Reverend S. McLeery, securely bound and gagged, in his study in Broad Street. He'd been there, he said, since 8.15 a.m., when two men had called and . . .

Enquiries in Newbury throughout the afternoon produced nothing. Nothing at all. And by tea-time everyone in the prison knew what had happened. It had not been Evans, impersonating McLeery, who had walked *out*; it had been Evans, impersonating McLeery, who had stayed *in*.

The fish and chips were delicious, and after a gentle stroll round the centre of Chipping Norton, Evans decided to return to the hotel and have an early night. A smart new hat concealed the wreckage of his closely cropped hair, and he kept it on as he walked up to the reception desk of the Golden Lion. It would take a good while for his hair to regain its former glories – but what the hell did *that* matter. He was *out* again, wasn't he? A bit of bad luck, that, when Jackson had pinched his scissors, for it had meant a long and tricky operation with his only razor blade the previous night. Ah! But he'd had his good luck, too. Just think! If Jackson had made him take his bobble hat off! Phew! That really *had* been a close call. Still, old Jackson wasn't such a bad fellow . . . One of the worst things – funny, really! – had been the beard. He'd always been allergic to sticking plaster, and even now his chin was irritatingly sore and red.

The receptionist wasn't the same girl who'd booked him in, but the change was definitely for the better. A real honey, this one. As he collected his key, he gave her his sexiest smile, told her he wouldn't be bothering with breakfast, ordered the *Daily Express*, and asked for an early-morning call at 6.45 a.m. Tomorrow was going to be another busy day.

He whistled softly to himself as he walked up the broad stairs . . . He'd sort of liked the idea of being dressed up as a minister – dog-collar and everything. Yes, it had been a jolly good idea for 'McLeery' to wear *two* black fronts, *two* collars. But that top collar! Phew! It had kept on slipping off the back stud; and there'd been that one panicky moment when 'McLeery' had only just got his hand up to his neck in time to stop the collars springing apart before Stephens . . . Ah! They'd got *that* little problem worked out all right, though: a pen stuck in the mouth whenever the evil eye had appeared at the peep-hole. Easy! But all that fiddling about under the blanket with the black front and the stud at the back of the collar – that had been far more difficult than they'd ever bargained for . . . Everything else had gone beautifully smoothly, though. In the car he'd found everything they'd promised him: soap and water, clothes, the map – yes, the *map*, of course. The Ordnance Survey Map of Oxfordshire . . . He'd got some good friends; some very clever friends. Christ, ah!

He unlocked his bedroom door and closed it quietly behind him – and then stood frozen to the spot, like a man who has just caught a glimpse of the Gorgon.

Sitting on the narrow bed was the very last man in the world that Evans had expected – or wanted – to see.

'It's not worth trying anything,' said the Governor quietly, as Evans's eyes darted desperately around the room. 'I've got men all round the place.' (Well, there were only *two*, really: but Evans needn't know that.) He let the words sink in. 'Women, too. Didn't you think the blonde girl in reception was rather sweet?'

Evans was visibly shaken. He sat down slowly in the only chair the small room could offer, and held his head between his hands. For several minutes there was utter silence.

Finally, he spoke. 'It was that bloody correction slip, I s'pose.'

'We-ell' (the Governor failed to mask the deep satisfaction

in his voice) 'there *are* a few people who know a little German.'

Slowly, very slowly, Evans relaxed. He was beaten – and he knew it. He sat up at last, and managed to smile ruefully. 'You know, it wasn't *really* a mistake. You see, we 'adn't been able to fix up any 'otel, but we could've worked that some other way. No. The really important thing was for the phone to ring just before the exam finished – to get the screws out of the way for a coupla minutes. So we 'ad to know exactly when the exam *started*, didn't we?'

'And, like a fool, I presented you with that little piece of information on a plate.'

'Well, *somebody* did. So, you see, sir, that correction slip killed two little birds with a single stone, didn't it? The name of the 'otel for *me*, and the exact time the exam started for, er, for, er . . .'

The Governor nodded. 'It's a pretty common word, though, "Löwe". It's on the beer labels for a start.'

'Good job it *is* pretty common, sir, or I'd never 'ave known where to come to, would I?'

'Nice name, though: *zum goldenen Löwen.*'

''Ow did you know which Golden Lion it was? There's 'undreds of 'em.'

'Same as you, Evans. Index number 313; Centre number 271. Remember? Six figures? And if you take an Ordnance Survey Map for Oxfordshire, you find that the six-figure reference 313/271 lands you bang in the middle of Chipping Norton.'

'Yea, you're right. Huh! We'd 'oped you'd bugger off to Newbury.'

'We did.'

'Well, that's something, I s'pose.'

'That question paper, Evans. Could you really understand all that German? I could hardly—'

'Nah! Course I couldn't. I knew *roughly* what it was all about, but we just 'oped it'd throw a few spanners in the works – you know, sort of muddle everybody a bit.'

The Governor stood up. 'Tell me one thing before we go. How on earth did you get all that blood to pour over your head?'

Evans suddenly looked a little happier. '*Clever*, sir. Very clever, that was – 'ow to get a couple o' pints of blood into a cell, eh? When there's none there to start off with, and when, er, and when the "invigilator", shall we say, gets searched before 'e comes in. Yes, sir. You can well ask about that, and I dunno if I ought to tell you. After all, I might want to use that particular—'

'Anything to do with a little rubber ring for piles, perhaps?'

Evans grinned feebly. 'Clever, though, wasn't it?'

'Must have been a tricky job sticking a couple of pints—'

'Nah! You've got it wrong, sir. No problem about *that*.'

'No?'

'Nah! It's the *clotting*, you see. That's the big trouble. We got the blood easy enough. Pig's blood, it was – from the slaughter'ouse in Kidlington. But to stop it clotting you've got to mix yer actual blood' (Evans took a breath) 'with one tenth of its own volume of 3.8 per cent trisodium citrate! Didn't know that, did you, sir?'

The Governor shook his head in a token of reluctant admiration. 'We learn something new every day, they tell me. Come on, m'lad.'

Evans made no show of resistance, and side by side the two men walked slowly down the stairs.

'Tell me, Evans. How did you manage to plan all this business? You've had no visitors – I've seen to that. You've had no letters—'

'I've got lots of friends, though.'

'What's that supposed to mean?'

'Me German teacher, for a start.'

'You mean—? But he was from the Technical College.'

'*Was* 'e?' Evans was almost enjoying it all now. 'Ever check up on 'im, sir?'

'God Almighty! There's far more going on than I—'

'Always will be, sir.'

'Everything ready?' asked the Governor as they stood by the reception desk.

'The van's out the front, sir,' said the pretty blonde receptionist. Evans winked at her; and she winked back at him. It almost made his day.

A silent prison officer handcuffed the recaptured Evans, and together the two men clambered awkwardly into the back seat of the prison van.

'See you soon, Evans.' It was almost as if the Governor were saying farewell to an old friend after a cocktail party.

'Cheerio, sir. I, er, I was just wonderin'. I know your German's pretty good, sir, but do you know any more o' these modern languages?'

'Not very well. Why?'

Evans settled himself comfortably on the back seat, and

grinned happily. 'Nothin', really. I just 'appened to notice that you've got some O-level Italian classes comin' up next September, that's all.'

'Perhaps you won't be with us next September, Evans.'

James Roderick Evans appeared to ponder the Governor's words deeply. 'No. P'r'aps I won't,' he said.

As the prison van turned right from Chipping Norton on to the Oxford road, the hitherto silent prison officer unlocked the handcuffs and leaned forward towards the driver. 'For Christ's sake get a *move* on! It won't take 'em long to find out—'

'Where do ye suggest we make for?' asked the driver, in a broad Scots accent.

'What about Newbury?' suggested Evans.

DEAD AS A DODO

> 'Why,' said the Dodo, 'the best way to explain it is to do
> it.' (And as you might like to try the thing yourself, some
> winter day, I will tell you how the Dodo managed it.)
>
> (Lewis Carroll, *Alice in Wonderland*)

It was more from necessity than from kindliness, just after 5 p.m. on a rain-soaked evening in early February 1990, that Chief Inspector Morse of the Thames Valley Police leaned over and opened the Jaguar's near-side door. One of his neighbours from the North Oxford bachelor flats was standing at the bus stop, was getting very wet – and was staring hard at him.

'Most kind!' said Philip Wise, inserting his kyphotic self into the passenger seat.

Morse grunted a vague acknowledgement as the car made a few further slow yards up the Banbury Road in the red-tail-lighted queue, his wipers clearing short-lived swaths across the screen. Only three-quarters of a mile to go, but at this time of day twenty minutes would be par for the progressively paralytic crawl to the flats. Never an easy conversationalist himself – indeed, known occasionally to lapse into total aphasia when driving a car – Morse was glad that Wise was doing all the talking. 'Something quite extraordinary's happened to me,' said the man in the dripping mackintosh.

In retrospect, Morse was aware that he'd listened, at least initially, with no more than polite passivity. But listen he had done.

*

Philip Wise had gone up to Exeter College, Oxford, in October 1938; and in due course his linguistic abilities (particularly in German) had ensured for him, when war broke out a year later, a cushy little job in an Intelligence Unit housed on the outskirts of Bicester. For two years he had lived there in a disagreeable and draughty Nissen-hut; and when the chance came of his taking digs back in Oxford, he'd jumped at it. Thus it was that in October 1941 he had moved into Crozier Road, a sunless thoroughfare just off the west of St Giles'; and it was there that he'd first met Miss Dodo Whitaker ('Only the one "t", Inspector') who had a tiny top-floor bedsitter immediately above his own room in the grimy four-storey property that stood at number 14.

Why on earth she'd been saddled with a name like 'Dodo', he'd never discovered – nor enquired; but she was certainly a considerably livelier specimen than the defunct *Didus ineptus* of Mauritius. Although physically hardly warranting any second glance, especially in the wartime 'Utility' boiler-suit she almost invariably wore, she had the inestimable merit of being interesting. And sometimes, over half a glass of mild beer in the ill-lit bar at the rear of the Bird and Baby, her wonted nervousness would disappear, and in her rather deep, husky voice she would talk with knowledge, volubility, and wit, about the class-structure, about the progress of the war – and about music. Yes, above all about music. The pair of them had joined the Record Library, thereafter spending a few candle-lit evenings together in Dodo's room listening to everything from Vivaldi to Wagner. On one occasion, Wise had almost been on the verge of telling her of the Platonic-plus pleasure he was beginning to experience in her company.

Almost.

Dodo had a brother called Ambrose who now and then managed to get a weekend leave-pass and come to stay with Dodo, usually (though quite unofficially) sleeping on the floor of her single room. Almost immediately, Philip Wise and Ambrose Whitaker became firm friends, spending (somewhat to Dodo's annoyance) rather too many hours together drinking whisky – a commodity plentiful enough, if over-priced, in the Bird and Baby, but a rare one in the wilds of Bodmin, where Ambrose, with two stripes on each arm, spent his days initiating recruits into the mysteries of antiquated artillery pieces. He was a winsome, albeit somewhat raffish, sort of fellow whose attraction to alcohol apparently eclipsed even his love of music (Dodo spoke of Ambrose, amongst other things, as a virtuoso on the piano). Those weekends had flashed by, with Wise far too soon finding himself walking across Gloucester Green to see his friend off at the Great Western station late on Sunday afternoons.

Brother and sister – what an engaging couple they were!

Rich, too – at least their parents were.

Dodo, in particular, made no secret of her parents' extremely comfortable lifestyle, which Wise himself had once (and only once) experienced at first hand, when Dodo had suggested – on his having to spend a week in Bristol in February 1942 – that he stayed with them; had even loaned him a key to the family mansion in case they were out when he arrived. Wise had already known that Dodo's parents lived in Bristol, since he'd noticed the post-mark on the letter (doubtless from Mummy) that lay each week on the undusted mahogany table in the small entrance hall of number 14 – her name in the address, incidentally, always prefixed by the

41

letter 'A'. Alice? Angela? Anne? Audrey? – Wise had never
been told and, again, had never enquired. But that little fact
was something else he'd known earlier, too, since he was with
her when, with a practised flourish of those slim and sinewy
fingers, she'd signed her membership card at the Record
Library. As for the parents, they turned out to be a straight-
laced, tight-faced pair who remained frigidly reserved
towards their guest throughout his short stay, and who
appeared less than effusively appreciative of Dodo – and
almost embarrassingly dismissive of Ambrose. Oddly, Wise
had not found a single fond memento of their talented
offspring in the Whitakers' gauntly luxurious villa, and not a
single family photograph to grace the daily-dusted
mantelpieces.

It was three weeks after his return from this ill-starred visit
that Dodo left Oxford, her wartime work (something 'hush-
hush', it was understood) necessitating a move to Chelten-
ham. Only about forty miles away – and she'd keep in touch,
she said.

But she hadn't.

'Forty-eight years ago, this was, Inspector. Forty-eight! I
was twenty-three myself, and she must have been about the
same. Year or two older, perhaps – I'm not sure. You see, I
never even asked her how old she was. Pretty spineless
specimen, wasn't I?'

In the darkness, Morse nodded his silent assent, and the
Jaguar finally turned into the Residents Only parking area.

Wise contrived to keep talking as the two men dashed
through the rain to the entrance hall. 'I'd be glad to give you

a cup of tea . . . or something . . . You see, I haven't really told you anything yet.'

As they sat opposite each other in the living area, Wise passed across a white, six-page booklet containing details of **A Service of Thanksgiving for the Life of AMBROSE WHITAKER, MA (Cantab.), FRAM 1917–1989**, and Morse glanced cursorily at the contents: music; hymn; lesson; music; address; prayers; hymn; music; blessing; music; more music. Observing only that if he ever had a voice in his own funeral arrangements he would join Whitaker in choosing the 'In Paradisum' from the Fauré *Requiem*, Morse handed the leaflet back.

'The thing is this,' continued Wise. 'I saw an obituary in *The Times* in December, and I was sure it was the same man I'd known in the war. Quite apart from the pretty unusual Christian name, as well as the *very* unusual spelling of the surname, everything else fitted, too: born in Bristol, prodigy on the piano – everything! And I just couldn't help thinking back and wondering whether *she* was still alive – Dodo, that is. Anyway, a fortnight ago I read about this Memorial Service in Holborn, and I decided to go up and pay my last respects to an old friend – and perhaps . . .'

'Find some plump-bosomed old spinster—'

'Yes!'

'Did you find her?' asked Morse quietly.

Wise shook his head. 'There were an awful lot of important people from the musical world – I hadn't realized what a name Ambrose had made for himself. I got to the church early and stayed outside for a good while watching the people going in, including – pretty obvious who she was – Ambrose's wife, who drew up in a chauffeur-driven Rolls – registration AW 1! But I didn't see the woman I was looking for – and she wasn't in the church, either. I'd have spotted her straight-away if she had been. She was smallish, stockily built – just like her mother. And there was something else. She had a nasty little red scar – well, a nasty *big* scar really – just across the left-hand side of her jaw: a bicycle accident when she was a youngster, I think. She was awfully conscious of it and always used a lot of face-powder to try to cover it up a bit. But it was still pretty noticeable, I'm afraid. Well, to cut a long story a bit shorter, I went up to Ambrose's wife after the service and told her I'd known her husband in the war and said how sorry I was and all the rest of it. She was pleasant enough, but she seemed a bit strained, and there were other people waiting to have a word with her. So I didn't say much more except to mention that I'd known her husband's sister as well.' Wise paused a second or two before continuing.

'Do you know what happened then, Inspector? Ambrose's wife pointed to a grey-haired woman in a black dress standing with her back to us, a woman very much the same height and build as Dodo had been. "This gentleman here says he used to know you, Agnes . . ."

'Agnes!

'But I didn't hear any more – I just didn't know what to do – or say. You see, the woman in black turned round and faced me, *and she wasn't Dodo Whitaker.*'

*

It was Morse who broke the silence which followed. 'Ambrose only had the one sister?'

Wise nodded, a wry, defeated smile upon his face. 'Yes – Agnes. He never did have a sister named "Dodo"!'

Again the two men were silent.

'Well?' asked Wise, finally.

It had always appeared to Morse an undeniable fact that coincidence plays a far greater role in human affairs than is generally acknowledged. And here was yet another instance of it – it must be! Wise's tale was interesting enough – assuredly so: but it wasn't much of a *problem*, surely? Ostentatiously he drained his whisky, gratefully witnessed the replenishment, and then pronounced judgement: 'There were two Ambrose Whitakers, both musical men, and both from Bristol, and the one you knew wasn't the one who died.'

'You think not?' The half-smile on Wise's face made Morse rather uncomfortably aware that a slightly more intelligent analysis had been expected of him.

'You don't think,' suggested Morse weakly, 'that Agnes might have had some plastic surgery or something?'

'No, no. It's just that there are far too many coincidences for *me* to swallow. *Everything* fitted – down to the last detail. For example, Dodo told me that she and Ambrose once got a bit morbid about the possibility of his being killed in the war and how he'd told her that he'd settle for a couple of bits of music when they buried him: the "In Paradisum"—'

'Lovely choice!' interjected Morse. 'I saw that in the Service.'

'—and the adagio from the Mozart Clarinet Concerto—'

'Ah yes! K662.'

'K622.'

'Oh!'

Morse knew that he wasn't scoring many points; knew, too, that Wise was perfectly correct in believing that the coincidences were getting way out of hand. But he had no time at all to develop the quite extraordinary possibility that suddenly leaped into his brain; because Wise himself was clearly most anxious to propound his own equally astonishing conclusions.

'What would you say, Inspector, if I told you that Dodo wasn't Ambrose Whitaker's sister at all – *she was his wife*.'

Morse's face registered a degree of genuine surprise, but he allowed Wise to continue without interruption.

'It would account for quite a few things, don't you think? For example, it always seemed a bit odd to me that when Ambrose got any leave he invariably came all the way from Cornwall here to Oxford – via *Bristol*, at that! – just to see his *sister*. You'd think he'd have called in on his parents once in a while, wouldn't you? They were much nearer than Dodo was; and well worth keeping the right side of, surely? But it wouldn't be surprising if he took every opportunity of coming all the way to Oxford to see his *wife*, would it? And that would certainly tie up with him sleeping in her room. You know, with all that family money he could have taken a suite in The Randolph if he'd wanted. Yet instead of that, he slept – or so he said – on Dodo's *floor*. Then again, it would probably account for the fact that she never once let me touch her physically – not even hold hands. She was fond of me, though – I know she was . . .'

Momentarily Wise stopped, nodding slowly to himself. 'For some reason the Whitakers must have disapproved of

Ambrose's marriage and wanted as little as possible to do with his wartime bride – hence their cool reception of me, Inspector! There may have been talk of disinheriting him – I don't know. I don't *know* anything, of course. But I suspect she was probably pregnant underneath that boiler-suit of hers, and as her time drew nearer she just *had* to leave Oxford. Then? Your guess is as good as mine: she died – she was killed in an air-raid – she got divorced – anything. Ambrose remarried, and the woman I met at the Memorial Service was his *second* wife.'

'Mm.' Morse was looking decidedly dubious. 'But if this Dodo girl *was* his wife, and if his parents couldn't stand the sight or sound of her, why on earth did they write to her every week? And why did she think she had the right to invite *you* down to Bristol? To *have* a key, even – let alone to give *you* one.' Morse shook his head slowly. 'She must have been pretty sure she could take their good-will for granted, I reckon.'

'You think they *were* her parents, then,' said Wise flatly.

'I'm sure of it,' said Morse.

Wise shook his head in exasperation. 'What the hell *is* the explanation, then?'

'Oh, I don't think there's much doubt about that,' said Morse. But he spoke these words to himself, and not to Wise. And very soon afterwards, seeing little prospect of any further replenishment, he took his leave – with the promise that he would give the problem 'a little consideration'.

The following Monday morning, Morse stood beside the Traffic Comptroller at Kidlington Police HQ and watched as

'AW 1' was keyed into the Car Registration computer. Immediately, the VDU spelled out the information that the car was still registered under the name of Mr A. Whitaker, 6 West View Crescent, Bournemouth; and noting the address Morse walked thoughtfully back to his ground-floor office. After ringing Directory Inquiries, and getting the Bournemouth telephone number, he was soon speaking to Mrs Whitaker herself, who in turn was soon promising to do exactly as Morse had requested.

Then Morse rang the War Office.

Ten days later, Philip Wise returned from a week's holiday in Spain to find a long note from Morse.

P. W.

I've discovered a few more facts, but some of what follows may possibly be pure fiction. As you know, records galore got destroyed in the last war, affording limitless opportunity for people to cover up their traces by means of others' identity-cards and so on, especially after a period of chaos and carnage when nobody knew who was who or which corpse was which.

After Dunkirk, for instance.

Gunner (as he then was) Whitaker was the only man of thirty on board who survived, quite miraculously, when the Edna (a flat-bottomed barge registered in Felixstowe) was blown out of the water by a German dive-bomber on May 30th, 1940. He was picked up, with only a pair of waterlogged pants and a wrist-watch to call his own, by the naval sloop Artemis, and was landed at Dover, along with tens of thousands of other soldiers from almost every regiment in the land. (My own imaginative faculties now come wholly into play.) In due course, he was put on a train and sent to a temporary rehabilitation camp – as it happened, the one here in Oxford up on Headington Hill.

The fact that he was in a state of profound shock, with his nerves half-shot to pieces, is probably sufficient to account for his walking out of this camp (quite literally) after only one night under canvas, and hitch-hiking down to Bristol. But he didn't walk out alone. He took a friend with him, a man from the same regiment; and they both quite deliberately got out of the camp before either could be re-documented and re-posted. This second man had only a mother and sister as close family, who were both killed in one of the very first air-raids on Plymouth; and for some (doubtless considerable) sum of money, donated by the protective Whitaker parents, this man agreed to leave on permanent record the official War Office version of his fate after Dunkirk – 'Missing presumed killed' – and for the rest of the war to assume the name and role of Ambrose Whitaker. In short, my guess is that the man who came up from Bodmin to see Dodo was not Ambrose Whitaker at all.

Your own guess about things fitted some of the facts well enough; but those facts also fit into a totally different pattern. Just consider some of them again. First, there was the weekly letter from Bristol, from parents who seemingly didn't even want to acknowledge their daughter and who hid all the family photos when you stayed with them. Odd! Then, take this daughter of theirs, Dodo. No great shakes physically, and only just up to attracting an impressionable young man after he'd had a few pints (please don't think me unfair!) in a dim pub-lounge or a candle-lit bedroom – yet she decided to hide whatever charms she'd got under a baggy boiler-suit. Decidedly odd! What else did you tell me about her? She was nervy; she had a deepish voice; she wore too much face-powder; she knew a great deal about the war ... (You've guessed the truth by now, I'm sure.) Her Christian name began with 'A', and you saw her sign her name that way at the Record Library – with the sinewy fingers of an executant musician. But that *wasn't* odd, was it? Her name *did* begin with 'A', and Ambrose Whitaker, as we know, was himself a fine pianist. And so it wasn't only the scar on her jaw she was anxious to conceal with those layers of face-powder – it was the stubble of a beard that grew there every day. Because Dodo Whitaker was a man! And not just any tuppeny-ha'penny old man, either: he was <u>Ambrose Whitaker</u>.

Two points remain to be cleared up. First, why was it necessary for Ambrose Whitaker to pose as a woman? Second, what was the relationship between Ambrose and the artillery corporal from Bodmin? On the first point, it's clear that if he wanted to avoid any further wartime traumas Ambrose couldn't stay in Bristol, where he was far too well known. Even if he moved to a place where he wasn't known, it wouldn't have been completely safe to move <u>as a man</u>; because suspicious questions were always going to be asked in wartime about a young fellow who looked as if he might well be dodging the column. So he took out a double insurance on his deception – for him a desperately needed deception – not only by moving to Oxford, but also by dressing and living <u>as a woman</u>. On the second point, we don't perhaps need to probe too deeply into the reasons why the sensitive and effeminate Ambrose was happy to take every opportunity of spending his nights with (forgive me!) the rather crude, whisky-swilling opportunist you got to know in the war. Such speculation is always a little distasteful, and I will say no more about it.

I rang Ambrose's widow, asking for a wartime photograph of her husband, and I gave her your address, telling her you are an archivist working for the Imperial War Museum. You should hear from her soon; and when you do you'll be as near as anyone is ever likely to be to knowing the truth about this curious affair.

E. M.

It was two days later that a still-pyjamaed Wise took delivery of a stiff white envelope, in which he found a brief note, together with a photograph of a young man in army uniform – a photograph in which no attempt had been made to turn the left-hand side of the sitter's face away from the honesty of the camera lens, or to retouch the line of a cruel scar that stretched across the face's lower jaw. And as Philip Wise looked down at the photograph he saw staring back at him the familiar, faithless eyes of Dodo Whitaker.

AT THE LULU-BAR MOTEL

> 'I am sorry I have not learnt to play at cards. It is very
> useful in life.'
>
> (Samuel Johnson, as reported by Boswell in
Tour to the Hebrides)

I shall never be able to forget what Louis said – chiefly, no
doubt, because he said it so often, a cynical smile slowly
softening that calculating old mouth of his: 'People are so
gullible!' – that's what he kept on saying, our Louis. And
I've used those selfsame words a thousand times myself –
used them again last night to this fat-walleted coach-load of
mine as they debussed at the Lulu-Bar Motel before tucking
their starched napkins over their legs and starting into one of
Louis' five-star four-coursers, with all the wines and a final
slim liqueur. Yes, people are so gullible ... Not *quite* all of
them (make no mistake!) – and please don't misunderstand
me. This particular manifestation of our human frailty is of
only marginal concern to me personally, since occasionally I
cut a thinnish slice of that great cake for myself – as I did
just before I unloaded those matching sets of leather cases
and hulked them round the motel corridors.

But let's get the chronology correct. All that hulking
around comes right after we've pulled into the motel where –
as always – I turn to all the good people (the black briefcase
tight under my right arm) and tell them we're here, folks;
here for the first-night stop on a wunnerful tour, which every
single one o' you is goin' to enjoy real great. From tomorrow
– and I'm real sorry about this, folks – you won't have me
personally lookin' after you any more; but that's how the
operation operates. I'm just the first-leg man myself, and

someone else'll have the real privilege of drivin' you out on the second leg post-breakfast. Tonight itself, though, I'll be hangin' around the cocktail bar (got that?), and if you've any problems about . . . well, about *anything*, you just come along and talk to me, and we'll sort things out real easy. One thing, folks. Just one small friendly word o' counsel to you all. There's one or two guys around these parts who are about as quick an' as slick an' as smooth as a well-soaped ferret. Now, the last thing I'd ever try to do is stop you enjoyin' your vaycaytions, and maybe one or two of you could fancy your chances with a deck o' cards against the deadliest dealer from here to Detroit. But . . . well, as I say, just a friendly word o' counsel, folks. Which is this: *some people are so gullible!* – and I just wouldn't like it if any o' you – well, as I say, I just wouldn't like it.

That's the way I usually dress it up, and not a bad little dressing up at that, as I think you'll agree. 'OK' (do I hear you say?) 'if some of them want to transfer their savings to someone else's account – so what? You can't live other folks' lives for them, now can you? You did your best, Danny boy. So forget it!' Which all makes good logical sense, as I know. But they still worry me a little – all those warm-hearted, clean-living folk, because – well, simply because they're so gullible. And if you don't relish reading about such pleasant folk who plop like juicy pears into the pockets of sharp-fingered charlatans – well, you're not going to like this story. You're not going to like it one little bit.

Most of them were in their sixties or early seventies (no children on the Luxi-Coach Package Tours), and as they filed past the old driving cushion they slipped me a few bucks each and thanked me for a real nice way to start a vaycaytion.

After that it took a couple of hours to hump all that baggage around the rooms, and it was half-past eight before I got down to some of Lucy's chicken curry. Lucy? She's a honey of a girl – the sort of big-breasted blonde that most of my fellow sinners would willingly seek to seduce and, to be honest with you . . . But let me return to the theme.

The cocktail bar is a flashily furnished, polychrome affair, with deep, full-patterned carpet, orange imitation-leather seats and soft wall-lighting in a low, pink glow; and by about half-past nine the place was beginning to fill up nicely. Quite a few of them I recognized from the coach: but there were others. Oh yes, there were a few others . . .

He wasn't a big fellow – five-six, five-seven – and he wore a loud check suit just like they used to do on the movies. When I walked in he was standing by the bar, a deck of cards shuttling magically from hand to hand. 'Fancy a game, folks? Lukey's the name.' He was pleasant enough, I suppose, in an ugly sort of way; and with his white teeth glinting in a broad-mouthed smile, you could almost stop disliking him. Sometimes.

It was just before ten when he got his first bite – a stocky, middle-aged fellow who looked as if he could take pretty good care of himself, thank you. So. So, I watched them idly as they sat opposite each other at one of the smooth-topped central tables, and it wasn't long before a few others began watching, too. It was a bit of interest – a bit of an incident. And it wasn't *their* money at stake.

Now Lukey loved one game above all others, and I'll have to bare its bones a bit if you're going to follow the story. (Be patient, please: we're running along quite nicely now.) First, it's a dollar stake in the kitty, all right? Then two cards are dealt to each of the players, the court cards counting ten, the ace eleven, and all the other cards living up to their marked face-value. Thus it follows, as day follows night and as luck follows Luke, that the gods are grinning at you if you pick up a ten and an ace – for that is vingt-et-un, my friends, whether you reckon by Fahrenheit or Centigrade, and twenty-one's the best they come. And so long as you remember not to break that twenty-one mile speed-limit, you can buy as many more cards as you like and . . . but I don't think you're going to have much trouble in following things.

It was the speed with which hand followed hand that surprised all the on-lookers, since our challenger ('Call me Bart') was clearly no stranger to the Lukesberry rules and five or six hands were through every minute. Slap! A dollar bill in the kitty. Slap! A dollar bill on top. Flick, flick; flick, flick; buy; stick; bust. Dollar, dollar; flick, flick; quicker, ever quicker. Soon I'm standing behind Barty and I can see his cards. He picks up a ten, and a four; and without mulling it over for a micro-second he says, 'Stick.' Then Lukey turns over a seven, and an eight – and then he flicks over another card for himself: a Jack. Over the top! And Barty pockets yet another kitty; and it's back to that dollar-dollar, flick-flicking again. And when Bart wins again, Luke asks him nicely if he'd like to deal. But Bart declines the kind offer. 'No,' he says. 'I'm on a nice li'l winnin' streak here, pal, so just you keep on dealing them pretty li'l beauties same as before – that's all I ask.'

So Lukey goes on doing just that; and by all that's supersonic what a sharp our Lukey is! I reckon you'd need more than a slow-motion replay to appreciate that prestissimo prestidigitation of his. You could watch those fingers with the eagle eye of old Cortes – and yet whether he was flicking the cards from the top or the middle or the bottom, I swear no one could ever tell. In spite of all this, though, Barty-boy is still advancing his winnings. Now he picks up a seven, and a four; and he decides to buy another card for ten dollars. So Lukey covers the ten dollars from his own fat roll, deals Barty a nine – and things are looking mighty good. Then Luke turns over his own pair (why he bothers, I can't really say, for he knows them all along): a six, and a nine, they are – and things look pretty bad. He turns over another card from the deck – an eight. And once more he's out of his dug-out and over the top.

'My luck'll change soon,' says Luke.

'Not with me, it won't,' says Bart, picking up the twenty-two dollars from the kitty.

'You quitting, you mean?'

'I'm quitting,' says Bart.

'You've played before, I reckon.'

'Yep.'

'You always quit when you're winning?'

'Yep.'

Luke says nothing for a few seconds. He just picks up the deck and looks at it sourly, as if something somewhere in the universe has gone mildly askew. Then he calls on the power of the poets and he quotes the only lines he's ever learned:

'Barty,' he says,

'"If you can make one heap of all your winnings
And risk it on one turn of pitch and toss . . ."'

Remember that? What about it? You've taken seventy-odd dollars off o' me, and I'm just suggestin' that if you put 'em in the middle – and if I cover 'em . . . What do you say? One hand, that's all.'

The audience was about thirty strong now, and as many were urging Barty *on* as were urging him *off*. And they were all pretty committed, too – one way or the other. One of them in particular . . .

I'd seen him earlier at the bar, and a quaint little fellow he was, too. By the look of him he was in his mid- or late-seventies, no more than four-ten, four-eleven, in his built-up shoes. His face was deeply tanned and just as deeply lined, and he wore a blazer gaudily striped in red and royal blue. Underneath the blazer pocket, tastelessly yet lovingly picked out in purple cotton, was the legend: Virgil K. Perkins Jnr. Which made you wonder whether Virgil K. Perkins Snr was still somewhere in circulation – although a further glance at his senile son seemed to settle that particular question in the negative. Well, it's this old-timer who tries pretty hard to get Bartey to pocket his dollars and call it a night. And for a little while it seemed that Barty was going to listen. But no. He's tempted – and he falls.

'Okey doke,' says Barty. 'One more hand it is.'

It was Luke now who seemed to look mildly uneasy as he covered the seventy-odd dollars and squared up the deck. From other parts of the room the crowd was rolling up in force again: forty, fifty of them now, watching in silence as Luke dealt the cards. Barty let his pair of cards lie on the table a few seconds and his hands seemed half full of the shakes as he picked them up. A ten; and a six. Sixteen. And for the first time that evening he hesitated, as he fell to figuring out the odds. Then he said, 'Stick'; but it took him twice to say it because the first 'stick' got sort of stuck in his larynx. So it was Lukey's turn now, and he slowly turned over a six – and then a nine. Fifteen. And Luke frowned a long time at his fifteen and his right hand toyed with the next card on the top of the deck, quarter turning it, half turning it, almost turning it – and then putting it back.

'Fifteen,' he said.

'*Sixteen,*' says Barty, and his voice was vibrant as he grabbed the pile of notes in the middle.

Then he was gone.

The on-lookers were beginning to drift away as Luke sat still in his seat, the cards still shuttling endlessly from one large palm to the other. It was the old boy who spoke to him first.

'You deserve a drink, sir!' he says. 'Virgil K. Perkins Junior's the name, and this is my li'l wife, Minny.'

'We're from Omaha,' says Minny dutifully.

And so Virgil gets Luke a rye whiskey, and they start talking.

'You a card player yourself, Mr Perkins?'

'Me? No, sir,' says Virgil. 'Me and the li'l wife here' (Minny was four or five inches the taller) 'were just startin' on a vaycaytion together, sir. We're from Omaha, just like she says.'

But the provenance of these proud citizens seemed of no great importance to Luke. 'A few quick hands, Mr Perkins?'

'No,' says Virgil, with a quiet smile.

'Look, Mr Perkins! I don't care – I just don't *care* – whether it's winnin' or losin', and that's the truth. Now if we just—'

'No!' says Virgil.

'You musta heard of beginner's luck?'

'*No!*' says Virgil.

'You're from Omaha, then?' says Luke, turning all pleasant-like to Minny . . .

I left them there, walked over to the bar, and bought an orange juice from Lucy, who sometimes comes through to serve about ten o'clock. She's wearing a lowly cut blouse, and a highly cute hair-style. But she says nothing to me; just winks – unsmilingly.

Sure enough, when I returned to the table, there was Virgil K. Perkins 'just tryin' a few hands', as he put it; and I don't really need to drag you through all the details, do I? It's all going to end up exactly as you expect . . . but perhaps I'd better put it down, if only for the record; and I'll make it all as brief as I can.

From the start it followed the usual pattern: a dollar up; a dollar down. Nice and easy, take it gently; and soon the little fellow was beaming broadly, and picking up his cards with accelerating eagerness. But, of course, the balance was slowly swinging against him: twenty dollars down; thirty; forty . . .

'Lucky little run for me,' says Luke with a disarming smile, as if for two dimes he'd shovel all his winnings across the table and ease that ever-tightening look round Virgil's mouth. It was all getting just a little obvious, too, and surely someone soon would notice those nimble fingers that forever flicked those eights and nines when only fours and fives could save old Virgil's day. And someone did.

'Why don't you let the old fella deal once in a while?' asks one.

'Yeah, why not?' asks another.

'You wanna deal, pop?' concedes Luke.

But Virgil shakes his white head. 'I've had enough,' he says. 'I shouldn't really—'

'Come on,' says Minny gently.

'He can deal. Sure he can, if he wants to,' says Luke.

'He can't deal off the bottom, though!'

Luke was on his feet in a flash, looking round the room. 'Who said that?' he asked, and his voice was tight and mean. All conversation had stopped, and no one was prepared to own up. Least of all me – who'd said it.

'Well,' said Luke, as he resumed his seat, 'that does it, pop! If I'm bein' accused of cheatin' by some lily-livered coward who won't repeat such villainous vilification – then we'll have to settle the question as a matter of honour, I reckon. *You* deal, pop!'

The old man hesitated – but not for too long. 'Honour' was one of those big words with a capital letter, and wasn't a thing you could shove around too lightly. So he picked up the cards and he shuffled them, boxing and botching the whole business with an awkwardness almost unmatched in the annals of card-play. But somehow he managed to square the deck – and he dealt.

'I'll buy one,' says Luke, slipping a ten-dollar bill into the middle.

Virgil slowly covers the stake, and then pushes over a card.

'Stick,' says Luke.

Taking from his blazer pocket an inordinately large handkerchief, the old man mops his brow and turns his own cards over: a queen; and – an ace!

Luke merely shrugs his shoulders and pushes the kitty across. 'That's the way to do it, pop! Just you keep dealing yourself a few hands like that and—'

'No!' cries Minny, who'd been bleating her forebodings intermittently from the very beginning.

But Virgil lays a gentle hand on her shoulder. 'Don't be cross with me, old girl. And don't *worry*! I'm just a-goin' to deal myself one more li'l hand and . . .'

And another, and another, and another. And the gods were not smiling on the little man from Omaha: not the slightest sign of the meanest grin. Was it merely a matter of saving Face? Of preserving Honour? No, sir! It seemed just plain desperation as the old boy chased his losses round and round that smooth-topped table, with Minny sitting there beside him, her eyes tightly closed as if she was pinning the remnants of her hopes in the power of silent prayer. (I hitched the briefcase tighter under my right arm as I caught sight of Lucy behind the crowd, her eyes holding mine – again unsmilingly.)

By half-past ten Virgil K. Perkins Jnr had lost one thousand dollars, and he sat there crumpled up inside his chair. It wasn't as if he was short of friends, for the large audience had been behind him all along, just willing the old fellow to win. And it wasn't as if anyone could blame our nimble-fingered Lukey any more, for it was Virgil himself who had long since been dealing out his own disasters.

Not any longer, though. He pushed the deck slowly across the table and stood up. 'I'm sorry, old girl,' he says to Minny, and his voice is all choked up. 'It was your money as much as mine . . .'

But Luke was leaning across and he put his mighty palm on the old boy's skinny wrist. And he speaks quietly. 'Look, pop! You've just lost yourself a thousand bucks, right? So I want you to listen to me carefully because I'm gonna tell you how we can put all that to rights again. Now, we'll just have one more hand—'

'NO!' (The little old lady's voice was loud and shrill this time.) 'He *won't*! He won't lay down another dollar, d'you hear me? He's just – he's just a poor old fool, can't you see that? He's just a gullible, poor old—' But the rest of her words were strangled in her throat, and Virgil sat down again and put his arm round her shoulder as she began to weep silently.

'Don't you *want* to get all your money back?' Luke's voice is quiet again, but everyone can hear his words.

'Don't listen to him!' shouts one.

'Call it a day, sir!' shouts another.

Says Luke, turning to all of them: 'Old pop, here, he's got one helluva sight more spunk in him than the rest o' you put together! And, what's more, not a single man jack o' you knows the proposition I'm proposin'. Well?' (Luke looks around real bold.) 'Well? *Do* you?'

It was all silence again now, as Luke looks across to Virgil and formulates his offer. 'Look, pop. I've been mighty lucky tonight, as I think you might agree. So, I'm going to give you the sort o' chance you'll never have again. And this is what we'll do. We'll have just one last hand and we'll take two points off my score. Got that? I pick up eighteen – we call it sixteen. And just the same whatever score it is. What do you say, pop?'

But old Virgil – he shakes his head. 'You're a good sport, Luke, but—'

'Let's make it *three* off then,' says Luke earnestly. 'I pick up twenty – we call it seventeen. OK? Look, pop!' (He leans across and grips the wrist again.) 'Nobody's *ever* gonna make you any better offer than that. *Nobody*. You know something?

It's virtually *certain* you're gonna get all that lovely money right back into that wallet o' yours, now, isn't it?'

It was tempting. Ye gods, it was tempting! And it was soon clear that the audience was thinking it was pretty tempting, too, with a good many of them revising their former estimate of things.

'What d'you say?' asks Luke.

'No,' says Virgil. 'It's not just me – it's Minny here. I've made enough of a fool of myself for one night, haven't I, old girl?'

Then Minny looked at him, straight on, like. A surprising change had come over her tear-stained face, and her blue eyes blazed with a sudden surge of almost joyous challenge. 'You take him on, Virgil!' she says, with a quiet, proud authority.

But Virgil still sat there dejected and indecisive. His hands ran across that shock of wavy white hair, and for a minute or two he pondered to himself. Then he decided. He took most of the remaining notes from his wallet, and counted them with lingering affection before stacking them neatly in the centre of the table. 'Do you wanna count 'em, Luke?' he says. And it was as if the tide had suddenly turned; as if the old man sensed the smell of victory in his nostrils.

For a few seconds now it seemed to be Luke who was nervy and hesitant, the brashness momentarily draining from him. But the offer had been taken up, and the fifty or sixty onlookers were in no mood to let him forget it. He slowly counted out his own bills, and placed them on the top of Virgil's.

Two thousand dollars – on one hand.

Luke has already picked up the deck, and now he's shuffling the spots with his usual, casual expertise.

'Why are *you* dealin'?'

Luke looks up, and stares me hard in the eye. 'Was that *you* just spoke, mister?'

I nod. 'Yep. It was me. And I wanna know why it is you think you got some goddam right to deal them cards – because you don't deal 'em straight, brother. You flick 'em off the top and you flick 'em off the bottom and for all I know you flick 'em—'

'I'll see you outside, mister, as soon as—'

'You'll do no such thing,' I replies quietly. 'I just ain't goin' to be outside no more tonight again – least of all for you, brother.'

He looked mighty dangerous then – but I just didn't care. The skin along his knuckles was growing white as he slowly got to his feet and moved his chair backwards. And then, just as slowly, he sat himself down again – and he surprises everybody. He pushes the deck over the table and he says: 'He's right, pop. *You* deal!'

Somehow old pop's shaking hands managed to shuffle the cards into some sort of shape; and when a couple of cards fall to the floor, it's me who bends down and hands them back to him.

'Cut,' says pop.

So Luke cuts – about halfway down the deck (though knowing Lukey I should think it was *exactly* halfway down). Miraculously, it seems, old Virgil's hands had gotten themselves rid of any shakes, and he deals the cards out firm and fine: one for Luke, one for himself; another for Luke, and another for himself. For a few moments each man left them lying there on the top of the table. Then Luke picks up his own – first the one, and then the other.

'Stick!' he says, and his voice is a bit hoarse.

Every eye in the room was now on Virgil as he turned over his first card – a seven; then the second card – a ten. Seventeen! And all you've got to do, my friends, is to add on three – and that's a handsome little twenty, and the whole room was mumbling and murmuring in approval.

Every eye now switches to Luke, and in the sudden tense silence the cards are slowly turned: first a king, and then – ye gods! – an ace! And as Lukey smiles down at that beautiful twenty-oner the audience groaned like they always do when its favourite show-jumper knocks the top off the last fence.

And where, my friends, do we go from there? Well, I'll tell you. It was Lucy who started it all immediately Luke had left. She pushed her way through the on-lookers and plunged her hand deep down between those glorious breasts of hers to clutch her evening's tips.

'Mr Perkins, isn't it? I know it isn't all that much; but – but if it'll help, please take it.' About seven or eight dollars, it was, no more – but, believe me, it bore its fruit two-hundred-fold. It was me who was next. I'd taken about thirty-five dollars on the coach and (once more hitching the old briefcase higher under my arm) I fished it all out of my back pocket and placed it a-top of Lucy's crumpled offerings.

'Mr Perkins,' I said sombrely. 'You should've been on *my* coach, old friend.' That's all I said.

As for Virgil, he said nothing. He just sat back all crumpled up like before, with Minny sobbing silently beside him. I reckon he looked as if he couldn't trust himself to say a single word. But it didn't matter. All the audience was sad and sullenly sympathetic – and, as I said, they'd had their fill of Louis' vintage wines. And I've got to hand it to them. Twenty dollars; another twenty dollars; a fifty; a few tens; another twenty; another fifty – I watched them all as these clean-living, God-fearing folk forked something from their careful savings. And I reckon there wasn't a single man-jack of them who didn't make his mark upon that ever-mounting pile. But still Virgil said nothing. When finally he stumbled his way to the exit, holding Minny in one hand and a very fat pile of other people's dollars in the other, he turned round as if he was going to say something to all his very good friends. But still the words wouldn't come, it seemed; and he turned once more and left the cocktail bar.

I woke late the next morning, and only then because Luke was leaning over me, gently shaking me by the shoulder.

'Louis says he wants to see you at half-past ten.'

I lifted my left arm and focused on the wrist-watch: already five to ten.

'You all right, Danny?' Luke was standing by the door now (he must have had a key for that!) and for some reason he didn't look mightily happy.

'Sure, sure!'

'Half-past, then,' repeated Luke, and closed the door behind him.

I still felt very tired, and I was conscious that the back of my head was aching – and that's unusual for me. Nothing to drink the night before – well, only the odd orange juice that Lucy had ... orange juice ... ? I fell to wondering slightly, and turned to look at the other side of the bed, where the sheet was neatly turned down in a white hypotenuse. Lucy had gone – doubtless gone early; but then Lucy was always sensible and careful about such things . . .

I saw my face frowning as I stood in front of the shaving-mirror; and I was still frowning when I took the suit off the hanger in the wardrobe and noticed that the briefcase was gone. But I'd have been frowning even more if the briefcase *hadn't* gone; and as I dressed, my head was clearing nicely. I picked up the two thick sealed envelopes that had nestled all night under my pillow, put them, one each, into the pockets of my overcoat, and felt happy enough when I knocked on the door of Louis' private suite and walked straight in. It was ten thirty-two.

There were the usual six chairs round the oblong table, and four of them were taken already: there was Luke, and there was Barty; then there was Minny; and at the head of the table, Louis himself – a Louis still, doubtless, no more than four-ten, four-eleven in his built-up shoes, but minus that garishly striped blazer now; minus, too, that shock of silvery hair which the previous evening had covered that large, bald dome of his.

'You're late,' he says, but not unpleasantly. 'Sit down, Danny.' So I sat down, feeling like a little boy in the first grade. (But I usually feel like that with Louis.)

'You seen Lucy?' asks Minny, as Barty pours me a drop of Irish.

'Lucy? No – have you tried her room?'

But no one seemed much willing to answer that one, and we waited for a few minutes in silence before Louis spoke again.

'Danny,' he says, 'you'll remember that when we brought you into our latest li'l operation a few months back I figured we'd go for about a quarter of a million before we launched out on a new one?'

I nodded.

'Well, we're near enough there now as makes no odds – a fact perhaps you may yourself be not completely unaware of? After all, Danny, it was one o' your jobs to take my li'l Lucy down to the bank on Mondays, now wasn't it? And I reckon you've got a pretty clear idea of how things are.'

I nodded again, and kept on looking him straight in the eyes.

'Well, it was never no secret from any of us – was it? – that I'd be transferrin' this li'l investment o' mine over to Luke and Bartholomew here as soon as they – well, as soon as they showed me they was worthy.'

I was nodding slowly all the time now; but he'd left something out. 'Lucy was goin' to be in it, too,' I said.

'You're very fond of my Lucy, aren't you?' says Minny quietly.

'Yep. I'm very fond of her, Minny.' And that was the truth.

'It's not bin difficult for any of us to see that, old girl, now has it?' Louis turned to Minny and patted her affectionately on the arm. Then he focuses on me again. 'You needn't have no worries about my li'l daughter, Danny. No worries at all! Did it never occur to you to wonder just why I christened this latest li'l investment o' mine as the "Lulu-Bar Motel"?'

For a few seconds I must have looked a little puzzled, but my head was clearing nicely with the whiskey, and I suddenly saw what he meant. Yes! What a deep old devil our Louis was! The *Lu*-cy, *Lu*-ke, *Bar*-tholomew Motel . . .

But Louis was still speaking: 'I only asked you down this mornin', Danny, because I was hopin' to wind it all up here and now – and to let you know how much I've bin aware o' your own li'l contribution. But – well, it's all tied up in a way with Lucy, isn't it? And I reckon' (he looked at Luke and Bart) 'I reckon we'd better call another li'l meeting tonight? About eight? All right?'

It seemed all right to all of us, and I got up to go.

'You off to town, Danny?' asks Louis, eyeing the overcoat.

'Yep.' That's all I said. Then I left them there and caught the bus to the station.

I'd always noticed it before: whenever I'd felt a bit guilty about anything it was as if I sensed that other people somehow seemed to *know*. But that's behind us now. And, anyway, it had been Lucy's idea originally – not mine. She'd needed me, of course, for devising the cheque and forging Louis' signature – for though I'm about as ham-fisted with a deck of cards as an arthritic octopus, I got my own particular specialism. Yes, sir! And Lucy trusted me, too, because I'd been carrying all that lovely money – 240,000 dollars of it! – all neatly stacked in five-hundred bills, all neatly enveloped and neatly sealed – why, I'd been carrying it all around with me in the old briefcase for two whole days! And Lucy – Lucy, my love! – we shall soon be meeting at the ticket barrier on number one platform – and then be drifting off together quietly in the twilight . . .

At a quarter to twelve I was there – standing in my overcoat and waiting happily. (Lucy had never been early in her life.) I lit another cigarette; then another. By twelve forty-five I was beginning to worry a little; by one forty-five I was beginning to worry a lot; and by two forty-five I was beginning to guess at the truth. Yet still I waited – waited and waited and waited. And, in a sense, I suppose, I've been waiting for Lucy ever since . . .

It was when the big hand on the station clock came round to four that I finally called it a day and walked over to look at the Departure Board. I found a train that was due for New York in forty-five minutes, and I thought that that had better be that. I walked into the buffet and sat down with a coffee. So? So, here was yet another of life's illusions lying shattered in the dust, and yet . . . Poor, poor, lovely Lucy! I nearly allowed myself a saddened little smile as I thought of her opening up those two big envelopes in the briefcase – and finding there those 480 pieces of crisp, new paper, each exactly the size of a 500-dollar bill. She must have thought I was pretty – well, pretty gullible, I suppose, when we'd both agreed that *she* should take away the briefcase . . .

A single to New York would cost about fifty or sixty dollars, I reckoned; and as I joined what seemed to be the shorter queue at the ticket office I took the bulky envelope from the right-hand pocket of the overcoat, opened it – and stood there stunned and gorgonized. Inside were about 240 pieces of crisp, new paper, each exactly the size of a 500-dollar bill; and my hands were trembling as I stood away from the queue and opened the other envelope. Exactly the same. Well, no – not *exactly* the same. On the top piece of blank paper there were three lines of writing in Louis' unmistakably minuscule hand:

I did my best to tell you Danny boy but you never did really understand that filosofy of mine now did you? It's just what I kept on telling you all along. People . . .

By now, though, I reckon you'll know those last few words that Louis wrote.

I walked back across to the buffet and ordered another coffee, counting up what I had in my pockets: just ten dollars and forty cents; and I fell to wondering where it was I went from here. Perhaps . . . perhaps there were one or two things in my favour. At least I could spell 'philosophy'; and then there was always the pretty big certainty (just as Louis said so often) that somewhere soon I'd find a few nice, kindly, gullible folk.

But as I glance around at the faces of my fellow men and women in the station buffet now, they all look very mean, and very hard.

NEIGHBOURHOOD
WATCH

Sed quis custodiet ipsos custodes?
(But what about the vigilantes? Who's going to watch after *them?*)

(Juvenal, *Satires*)

'We must never make the criminal the *hero*, though!' proclaimed Marcus Price, Fellow of All Souls, as he drained his beer and put down his glass with the gesture of a man announcing to the company that *he'd* bought the previous round himself and whose turn, pray, was it now.

'What about old Raffles, though? Gentleman-burglar and all that. Remember him?'

The speaker was another Oxford don, Denis Stockman, an authority (*the* authority) on the Grand Duchy of Lithuania in the fifteenth century.

'Stole the Crown Jewels or something,' Stockman continued, 'then took 'em back when he found out what they were. No chivalry like that these days, eh, Morse?'

'Oh no,' mumbled Morse.

Oh dear! But Morse had only himself to blame. He'd meant to nip into the King's Arms just briefly that Wednesday lunchtime; and for a start things had looked promising. The one other customer was a very attractive thirty-odd-year-old brunette with sludgy green eyes. She had smiled momentarily as he'd sat down a few feet from her – before turning her attention back to *The Times* crossword puzzle, in which even as he took his first draught she wrote another word, with her left hand, the middle fingernail marked with a broad, white lateral line, as if she might have trapped it in a door.

Yes, only himself to blame . . .

Almost as soon as they'd spotted him there they'd pounced. *How* long is it? Mind if we *join* you? What are you *drinking*? Morse should, of course, have pleaded urgency in some criminal pursuit. But he didn't. The prospect of a further pint gladdened his heart, and he heard himself saying, 'Best Bitter.'

It was the fourth member of the quartet who now volunteered to get in the second round of drinks – a small, bald-headed man with a beer-belly and an NHS hearing-aid in his right ear. Morse had met him once or twice before and recalled that he'd been a refugee from pre-war Germany who now lived (very near Morse, wasn't it?) in a large North Oxford property reputedly stuffed with eminently collectable furniture and ornaments. Yes! Dr Eric Ullman – that was his name! A bachelor – like Morse.

'Good health, gentlemen!' Ullman's diction was precise, pedantic almost, as he raised his glass and toasted his two university acquaintances – and the chief inspector. 'And please forgive me perhaps if I tell you something – well, something that may surprise you a little?'

If any of the three pairs of eyebrows raised themselves, it was by little more than a millimetre.

'You're wrong, I think,' began Ullman, 'about there being no honour among thieves these days. Please let me explain. Last Friday I went to see *Così fan Tutte* at the Apollo Theatre here in Oxford. The Welsh National were doing it – doing it this week too, as you'll know. I got home at about a quarter past eleven, and most foolishly I didn't bother to put my car away in the garage. Next morning, when I looked out of the window? The drive was completely empty. The car was gone!'

'Metro, wasn't it?' asked Price.

Ullman nodded. 'I've had it for nine years.'

Stockman coughed slightly. 'Was it *worth* pinching, Eric?'

'It was worth a lot to me,' said Ullman simply.

Price grinned. 'Three hundred quid – in part exchange? No more.'

'You didn't *hear* anything?' asked Morse.

'No. And shall I tell you something else? They'd even closed the gates behind them.'

'Probably *pushed* it out of the drive,' suggested Morse. 'Saves any noise. And you're only a couple of hundred yards from the Ring Road . . .'

'I suppose so.'

'Did you ring us? Ring the police?'

'Straightaway. It would probably turn up in three or four days, they said. Out on one of the estates – minus wheels, minus radio, minus anything detachable – panels kicked in – windows smashed . . .'

'Bloody *mind*-less, isn't it!' Price shook his head vehemently. 'I know what I'd give some of these young sods – and it *wouldn't* be a few gentle hours of community service!'

'Just – just a minute.' Ullman raised his right hand, and the others were silent again. 'You see, they *didn't* find it out in East Oxford. Oh no. Three days went by, and then on Monday – last Monday – I was invited out to dinner at The Randolph. And when I got back, about eleven or so, there – there in the drive . . .'

Ullman was telling his little tale well, and three pairs of eyes now betrayed an unexpected interest.

'. . . completely undamaged – in fact looking *very* spick-and-span. And under the windscreen wiper – this!'

From his breast-pocket he took out a letter, a letter written in a small, neat, upright script, with no address, no date, no salutation, no valediction; a letter which each of Ullman's immediate audience now read in turn:

> Sorry about the inconvenience – very sorry indeed. I just had to have a car and your's was there. Its had a shampoo and I filled the petrol tank – unleaded, like it says in the handbook. Your little car saved my bacon, that's the truth, and I'm grateful. Please then do me the honour of accepting the enclosed ticket. I know you enjoy opera. I wasn't sure what performance to choose but Wagner is king for me, and in my opinion Die Valkurie is the greatest thing he ever wrote. Enjoy your evening, and thanks again.

Morse was the last to read the letter, his face betraying some slight puzzlement – as Ullman produced a ticket for the following Friday's performance.

£40!

Phew!

'Is it genuine?' queried Stockman.

' "Ring-side" seat, if you see what I mean,' replied Ullman.

Morse smiled gently at the little man's pleasantry as he held the ticket up to the light and pretended to be checking a possible irregularity of watermark.

'Genuine enough, I reckon,' he said, wishing dearly that the ticket was his own.

Beer glasses were empty again now, and Morse decided that it was either him or Stockman for the next round.

Let it be Stockman!

The back bar was a popular venue – ill-designed, intimate, awkward – and was now almost full this mid-lunchtime as Morse excused his premature departure and carefully squeezed his way past the woman to his right. Apparently she had been paying more attention to Ullman than to her crossword puzzle, for as far as Morse could see she had made very little, if any, progress.

And indeed Morse was right. Like most of the other customers there she had been very interested in Ullman's tale; interested in one or two other things as well. Had anyone apart from herself, for example, noticed that Morse (inadvertently?) had forgotten to hand back to Ullman the letter from the car thief? Had anyone apart from herself observed the conspiratorial exchange of glances between the two of them – between the man the others called Morse and Ullman himself? 'Conspiratorial'? No, that was too strong a word for it, perhaps. But something *like* that had been there. She could have sworn it.

Interesting!

There was something else too. After Morse had left, the little man's eyes had caught hers – almost as if she might have been a vague acquaintance. Not that she was: she'd never seen him in her life before. But she thought there'd been something almost . . . sinister about his look. 'Sinister'? Yes, that *wasn't* too strong a word for it. It was as if he knew something about her that she hardly knew herself.

Morse sauntered around Blackwell's for half an hour before walking over to the bus stop in Cornmarket. On the ride back to Kidlington he read the letter twice more, reflecting yet again on the bizarre coincidence that a car thief – a car thief! – should share his own highly idiosyncratic view about the greatest opera ever composed . . . Reflecting also on just those two (forgivable?) lapses in English grammar; and on that one (wholly unforgivable!) lapse which still puzzled Morse sorely as he walked up the incline to Police HQ.

'Nice, er, lunch, sir?' Lewis broke off his typing and looked down at his wrist-watch.

'Shut up and listen! Chap has his car pinched – OK? Few days later it's returned, in better nick than when it was pinched – with a note saying very sorry but I had to have a car and to make up for all the trouble here's an expensive ticket for the opera. You with me?'

Lewis nodded.

'So this chap goes along to the opera and when he gets back home—'

'He finds he's been burgled,' said Lewis flatly.

'You been sleeping in the knife-box?'

'No. Heard of it before, sir. There was a case like that a few weeks ago out in High Wycombe – so one of the lads was saying.'

'Oh!'

'Sorry to disappoint you, sir.'

'You think many other people have heard of it?'

'Doubt it. Not the sort of thing you want broadcasting, is it? I mean, you'd probably get lots of copy-cat crimes. For a start anyway.'

'Mm.'

'Clever though.'

'Bloody clever!'

'Why did you mention it, sir?'

Morse grinned. 'What are you doing on Friday evening?'

'Not sure. The wife's got a Tupperware party, I think,
but—'

'Would you be glad to get away?'

It was Lewis's turn to grin. 'What time do you want me?'

It was at one minute past seven, from the front seats of a
white Self Hire van, that the pair of them saw the man leave
his property and walk briskly away.

'You're a *very* clever bugger to think of this, you know,
Millie!'

'Don't count your chickens – not yet.'

'No – plenty o' time.'

'Three and a half hours – Christ!'

'More'n two football matches.'

'You're a philistine, Charlie!'

'What me? Don't be daft. Wagner's me greatest passion in
life, didna tell yer?'

It was from their unmarked car that Morse and Lewis
observed Ullman leave on foot. With a new alarm system
fitted, and with a stout Krooklok fixed between steering-
wheel and clutch, the Metro was now safely housed in the
bolted garage. Clearly Ullman was taking no further risks;
and in any case, buses were fairly frequent down the Banbury
Road – down to the City Centre – down to the Apollo
Theatre.

At half-past eight, Lewis ventured his first criticism:

'What time do you say this thing started?'

'Give 'em a *chance*, Lewis! They've got till midnight, near as dammit.'

'But we've already been here—'

'Ssshhh!' hissed Morse as a strong-bodied woman walked up the gravel drive to Ullman's front door, looked around with some interest – before pushing what appeared to be a free newspaper into the letter-box; then retracing her steps, and closing the gate to the drive behind her.

'Exciting little incident, wouldn't you say, sir?' asked Lewis wearily.

But Morse refused to rise to the bait.

At ten minutes past nine, a man opened the drive gate, closed it behind him, and walked up to the front door, where he looked over his shoulder for a good many seconds as if almost expecting to see someone, before extracting the newspaper from the letter-box, finding a key, and entering the house.

Dr Eric Ullman.

Morse was still shaking his head a quarter of an hour later when Lewis came back from the bar at the Dew Drop in Summertown with a pint of Best Bitter, and half a glass of Beamish.

'He might just have got fed up with it, sir? Not everybody's cup o' tea – Wagner.'

'It's *his* cup o' tea though: that's the whole point. No, there's something very wrong somewhere, I'm sure of it,

Lewis. They must've *known* he'd come back early . . . They must have got wind of it somehow.'

'Perhaps Dr Ullman guessed – well, what *you* guessed, sir?'

'Ye-es! Do you know, I think you may be right.' Morse took out the letter yet again. 'You see, whoever wrote this says he's a great Wagner fan, agreed?'

'Like you.'

'Like me, yes. But I don't believe him. Look!' Morse jabbed a forefinger at two words in the letter: 'Die Valkurie'.

Lewis looked appropriately vague. 'All German to me, sir.'

Morse tried to smile. 'Oh no, Lewis! That, if I may say so, is precisely the point. It *isn't* German! If you spend your life with anything – if you read about it – if you think about it – if you play it time and time again—'

'Like you.'

'Like me, yes.'

'I'm still not—'

'He can't even *spell* the bloody word!'

'We all make the occasional spelling mistake—'

'What? Three spelling mistakes in one word? *Three?* Come off it! He spells it with a "V" instead of a "W"; he sticks a spurious "i" in before the "e"; and he misses the umlaut off the "u"—'

'The what, sir?'

Morse peeled the back off a beer-mat and wrote out the correct spelling of the opera: 'Die Walküre'.

'Ullman's a German though, isn't he?' asked Lewis slowly.

'German origin, yes.'

'So why . . . why didn't *he* notice, well – what you noticed?'

'I'm beginning to think he did, Lewis. I'm beginning to think he did.'

'But you still felt pretty certain that Dr Ullman was going to be burgled tonight?'

'If I'd felt all *that* certain, I'd have had a few heavies round the corner in a police van.'

'Well, at least he's still got all that valuable furniture of his – that's one good thing.'

'That's one way of looking at it.'

'You got anything valuable in the furniture line yourself, sir?'

'Me? Oh, just the one piece, that's all. The family heirloom – nest of tables – Chippendale – 1756. What about you?'

'Just the big mahogany wardrobe – Utility – 1942. We've been trying to give it away this last year but nobody seems to appreciate the quality.'

Lewis drove the two of them back up to North Oxford, where on Morse's instruction they stopped for a brief while outside Ullman's residence once again. And even as they watched, the small portly figure of Eric Ullman passed across the uncurtained window of the lighted front room.

'If he's been burgled tonight, I'm a Dutchman,' volunteered Lewis.

But Lewis was no Dutchman, Morse knew that. 'You get off home, Lewis. I'll walk from here.'

'You sure, sir? It must be all of three hundred yards.'

'Less of the sarcasm, Sergeant!'

'Night, sir.'

•

Morse had put out his two Co-op semi-skimmed milk tokens, and was pouring himself a touch of the malt – when he suddenly knew that something was terribly wrong. Why hadn't he spotted the short note on the kitchen table immediately?

> Sorry about the inconvenience – very sorry indeed. It was the only thing you'd got worth pinching though and I'm hoping I'll get a good price.

That was all.

Morse bounded up the stairs, where on the landing he surveyed the empty square of unhoovered carpet upon which, until so very recently, had stood the one *objet d'art* that had been passed down from one generation of the Morse clan to the next – the family heirloom – the nest of tables – Chippendale – 1756.

It was Sergeant Dixon on night duty. 'Thank goodness you've rung, sir. We've been trying to get you but your phone's not been answering—'

'I've been *out*, man! You don't *mind*, do you?'

'Course not. It's just that you've had burglars, I'm afraid—'

'That's exactly what I'm ringing to tell you!'

'No need to worry though, sir. They didn't pinch anything. We've caught 'em – the pair of 'em.'

'You've done *what*?'

'You see this fellow rang us and said there was somebody in your flat, but when our boys got there they'd scarpered.

This fellow'd got the number though – white Self Hire van – and we stopped it out on the A40 near Wheatley. Just a few old tables in the back – don't think they could've taken anything of yours, sir. They must have got wind of us somehow, I reckon.'

'Who *was* this fellow?'

'A Dr Ullman, sir – lives quite near you, so he said.'

Morse was shaking his head yet again as he put down the phone. Everything – almost everything – was becoming clear at long last. The same thought must have struck the two of them, both himself and Ullman, in the King's Arms that lunchtime; the same strange thought that far from being a gesture of courtesy and gratitude, the letter and the opera ticket were merely the appropriate stages in a subtle strategy of deception.

Yes!

And Morse's thinking had gone one step further.

And Ullman's thinking had gone *two* steps further.

Morse locked his front door very carefully behind him and walked out into the night.

'A wee drop of the malt, Chief Inspector?'

'Excellent!'

'I was hardly expecting you *tonight*.'

'Did you ever think of joining the police force, Doctor?'

'I'm not tall enough.'

'You were always a move or so ahead of me!'

'Ah! But to be honest with you I *did* have one little

advantage over you. I've got a pair of wrens nesting in the front garden, you see, and I was watching them through the field-glasses recently when I noticed a woman, at the bus stop just outside; and I could see that *she* was watching something too – watching the house, the drive, the garage . . . Then two days later I saw her again, and I looked at her *very* closely through the field-glasses and I could see she was copying something down in a red notebook, writing with her left hand – and I noticed that she had a white scar on the nail of her middle finger, as if she'd trapped it in a door. And then I saw her *again*, didn't I . . .?'

Ullman smiled, and as he did so his features momentarily took on an almost sinister appearance.

'And you felt pretty certain that it was *me* who was going to get burgled tonight,' said Morse slowly.

'It seemed logical, yes. After all, if you were watching *my* property, you couldn't be watching your own as well, now could you?'

'You took a huge risk though.'

'You think so?' The little man appeared puzzled.

'Well, if they burgled *you*, while you were round at my place watching *me* . . .'

'Oh no. I've finished taking risks, you see. The private detective I hired to keep a look-out here was the very best in the business, so they told me: black belt at judo, Lord knows what else.'

'He must have been pretty good – we certainly didn't spot him.'

'*Her*, Chief Inspector. She said she'd probably do her "free-newspaper-delivery" routine—'

'Bloody 'ell!' mumbled Morse to himself.

'—and I told her she could pack it in for the night just after I'd rung the police – just before I got back here – about nine o'clock.'

'Ten past nine, to be accurate – that's when we spotted you.'

'Er' – Ullman coughed modestly and drained his malt – 'if we're to be accurate, Chief Inspector, shouldn't it be when *we* spotted *you*?'

For the last time that day Morse shook his head. Then draining his own glass and making his farewell, slowly he walked the three hundred yards back home.

A CASE OF
MIS-IDENTITY

His friend and foil, the stolid Watson with whom he shares rooms in Baker Street, attends Holmes throughout most of his adventures.

(*The Oxford Companion to English Literature*)

Long as had been my acquaintance with Sherlock Holmes, I had seldom heard him refer to his early life; and the only knowledge I ever gleaned of his family history sprang from the rare visits of his famous brother, Mycroft. On such occasions, our visitor invariably addressed me with courtesy, but also (let me be honest!) with some little condescension. He was – this much I knew – by some seven years the senior in age to my great friend, and was a founder member of the Diogenes Club, that peculiar institution whose members are ever forbidden to converse with one another. Physically, Mycroft was stouter than his brother (I put the matter in as kindly a manner as possible); but the single most striking feature about him was the piercing intelligence of his eyes – greyish eyes which appeared to see beyond the range of normal mortals. Holmes himself had commented upon this last point: 'My dear Watson, you have recorded – and I am flattered by it – something of my own powers of observation and deduction. Know, however, that Mycroft has a degree of observation somewhat the equal of my own; and as for deduction, he has a brain that is unrivalled *virtually* unrivalled – in the northern hemisphere. You may be relieved, however, to learn that he is a trifle lazy, and quite decidedly somnolent – and that his executant ability on the violin is immeasurably inferior to my own.'

(Was there, I occasionally wondered, just the hint of competitive envy between those two unprecedented intellects?)

I had just called at 221B Baker Street on a fog-laden November afternoon in 188–, after taking part in some research at St Thomas's Hospital into suppurative tonsilitis (I had earlier acquainted Holmes with the particulars). Mycroft was staying with Holmes for a few days, and as I entered that well-known sitting room I caught the tail-end of the brothers' conversation.

'Possibly, Sherlock – possibly. But it is the *detail*, is it not? Give me all the evidence and it is just possible that I could match your own analyses from my corner armchair. But to be required to rush hither and thither, to find and examine witnesses, to lie along the carpet with a lens held firmly to my failing sight . . . No! It is not my *métier*.'

During this time Holmes himself had been standing before the window, gazing down into the neutral-tinted London street. And looking over his shoulder I could see that on the pavement opposite there stood an attractive young woman draped in a heavy fur coat. She had clearly just arrived, and every few seconds was looking up to Holmes's window in hesitant fashion, her fingers fidgeting with the buttons of her gloves. On a sudden she crossed the street, and Mrs Hudson was soon ushering in our latest client.

After handing her coat to Holmes, the young lady sat nervously on the edge of the nearest armchair, and announced herself as Miss Charlotte van Allen. Mycroft nodded briefly at the newcomer, before reverting to a monograph on polyphonic plainchant; whilst Holmes himself made observation of the lady in that abstracted yet intense manner which was wholly peculiar to him.

'Do you not find,' began Holmes, 'that with your short sight it is a little difficult to engage in so much type-writing?'

Surprise, apprehension, appreciation, showed by turns upon her face, succeeded in all by a winsome smile as she appeared to acknowledge Holmes's quite extraordinary powers.

'Perhaps you will also tell me,' continued he, 'why it is that you came from home in such a great hurry?'

For a few seconds, Miss van Allen sat shaking her head with incredulity; then, as Holmes sat staring towards the ceiling, she began her remarkable narrative.

'Yes, I did bang out of the house, because it made me very angry to see the way my father, Mr Wyndham, took the whole business – refusing even to countenance the idea of going to the police, and quite certainly ruling out any recourse to yourself, Mr Holmes! He just kept repeating – and I *do* see his point – that no real harm has been done . . . although he can have no idea of the misery I have had to endure.'

'Your father?' queried Holmes quietly. 'Perhaps you refer to your step-father, since the names are different?'

'Yes,' she confessed, 'my step-father. I don't know why I keep referring to him as "father" – especially since he is but five years older than myself.'

'Your mother – she is still living?'

'Oh, yes! Though I will not pretend I was over-pleased when she remarried so soon after my father's death – and then to a man almost seventeen years younger than herself. Father – my real father, that is – had a plumbing business in the Tottenham Court Road, and Mother carried on the company after he died, until she married Mr Wyndham. I think he considered such things a little beneath his new wife, especially with his being in a rather superior position as a traveller in French wines. Whatever the case, though, he made Mother sell out.'

'Did you yourself derive any income from the sale of your father's business?'

'No. But I do have £100 annual income in my own right; as well as the extra I make from my typing. If I may say so, Mr Holmes, you might be surprised how many of the local businesses – including Cook and Marchant – ask me to work for them a few hours each week. You see' (she looked at us with a shy, endearing diffidence) 'I'm quite good at *that* in life, if nothing else.'

'You must then have some profitable government stock—?' began Holmes.

She smiled again. 'New Zealand, at four and a half per cent.'

'Please forgive me, Miss van Allen, but could not a single lady get by very nicely these days on – let us say, fifty pounds per annum?'

'Oh, certainly! And I myself live comfortably on but ten shillings per week, which is only half of that amount. You see, I never touch a single penny of my inheritance. Since I live at home, I cannot bear the thought of being a burden to my parents, and we have reached an arrangement whereby Mr Wyndham himself is empowered to draw my interest each quarter for as long as I remain in that household.'

Holmes nodded. 'Why have you come to see me?' he asked bluntly.

A flush stole over Miss van Allen's face and she plucked nervously at a small handkerchief drawn from her bag as she stated her errand with earnest simplicity. 'I would give everything I have to know what has become of Mr Horatio Darvill. There! Now you have it.'

'Please, could you perhaps begin at the beginning?' encouraged Holmes gently.

'Whilst my father was alive, sir, we always received tickets for the gas-fitters' ball. And after he died, the tickets were sent to my mother. But neither Mother nor I ever thought of going, because it was made plain to us that Mr Wyndham did not approve. He believed that the class of folk invited to such gatherings was inferior; and furthermore he asserted that neither of us – without considerable extra expenditure – had anything fit to wear. But believe me, Mr Holmes, I myself had the purple plush that I had never so much as taken from the drawer!'

It was after a decent interval that Holmes observed quietly: 'But you *did* go to the ball?'

'Yes. In the finish, we both went – Mother and I – when my step-father had been called away to France.'

'And it was there that you met Mr Horatio Darvill?'

'Yes! And – do you know? – he called the very next morning. And several times after that, whilst my step-father was in France, we walked out together.'

'Mr Wyndham must have been annoyed once he learned what had occurred?'

Miss van Allen hung her pretty head. 'Most annoyed, I'm afraid, for it became immediately clear that he did not approve of Mr Darvill.'

'Why do you think that was so?'

'I am fairly sure he thought Mr Darvill was interested only in my inheritance.'

'Did Mr Darvill not attempt to keep seeing you – in spite of these difficulties?'

'Oh yes! I thought, though, it would be wiser for us to stop seeing each other for a while. But he did write – every single day. And always, in the mornings, I used to receive the letters myself so that no one else should know.'

'Were you engaged to this gentleman?'

'Yes! For there was no problem about his supporting me. He was a cashier in a firm in Leadenhall Street—'

'Ah! Which office was that?' I interposed, for that particular area is known to me well, and I hoped that I might perhaps be of some assistance in the current investigation. Yet the look on Holmes's face was one of some annoyance, and I sank further into my chair as the interview progressed.

'I never did know exactly which firm it was,' admitted Miss van Allen.

'But where did he live?' persisted Holmes.

'He told me that he usually slept in a flat on the firm's premises.'

'You must yourself have written to this man, to whom you had agreed to become engaged?'

She nodded: 'To the Leadenhall Street Post Office, where I left my letters *poste restante*. Horatio – Mr Darvill – said that if I wrote to him at his work address, he'd never get to see my envelopes first, and the young clerks there would be sure to tease him about things.'

It was at this point that I was suddenly conscious of certain stertorous noises from Mycroft's corner – a wholly reprehensible lapse into poor manners, as it appeared to me.

'What else can you tell me about Mr Darvill?' asked Holmes quickly.

'He was very shy. He always preferred to walk out with me in the evening than in the daylight. "Retiring", perhaps, is the best word to describe him – even his voice. He'd had the quinsy as a young man, and was still having treatment for it. But the disability had left him with a weak larynx, and a sort of whispering fashion of speaking. His eyesight, too, was rather feeble – just as mine is – and he always wore tinted spectacles to protect his eyes against the glare of any bright light.'

Holmes nodded his understanding; and I began to sense a note of suppressed excitement in his voice.

'What next?'

'He called at the house the very evening on which Mr Wyndham next departed for France, and he proposed that we should marry before my step-father returned. He was convinced that this would be our only chance; and he was so dreadfully in earnest that he made me swear, with my hand upon both Testaments, that whatever happened I would always be true and faithful to him.'

'Your mother was aware of what was taking place?'

'Oh, *yes*. And she approved so much. In a strange way, she was even fonder of my fiancé than I was myself, and she agreed that our only chance was to arrange a secret marriage.'

'The wedding was to be in church?'

'Last Friday, at St Saviour's, near King's Cross; and we were to go on to a wedding-breakfast afterwards at the St Pancras Hotel. Horatio called a hansom for us, and put Mother and me into it before stepping himself into a four-wheeler which happened to be in the street. Mother and I got to St Saviour's first – it was only a few minutes' distance away. But when the four-wheeler drove up and we waited for him to step out – he never did, Mr Holmes! And when the cabman got down from the box and looked inside the carriage – *it was empty.*'

'You have neither seen nor heard of Mr Darvill since?'

'Nothing,' she whispered.

'You had planned a honeymoon, I suppose?'

'We had planned,' said Miss van Allen, biting her lip and scarce managing her reply, 'a fortnight's stay at the Royal Gleneagles in Inverness, and we were to have caught the lunchtime express from King's Cross.'

'It seems to me,' said Holmes, with some feeling, 'that you have been most shamefully treated, dear lady.'

But Miss van Allen would hear nothing against her loved one, and protested spiritedly: 'Oh, no, sir! He was far too good and kind to treat me so.'

'Your own opinion, then,' said Holmes, 'is that some unforeseen accident or catastrophe has occurred?'

She nodded her agreement. 'And I think he must have had some premonition that very morning of possible danger, because he begged me then, once again, to remain true to him – whatever happened.'

'You have no idea what that danger may have been?'

'None.'

'How did your mother take this sudden disappearance?'

'She was naturally awfully worried at first. But then she became more and more angry; and she made me promise never to speak to her of the matter again.'

'And your step-father?'

'He seemed – it was strange, really – rather more sympathetic than Mother. At least he was willing to discuss it.'

'And what was his opinion?'

'He agreed that some accident must have happened. As he said, Mr Darvill could have no possible interest in bringing me to the very doors of St Saviour's – and then in deserting me there. If he had borrowed money – or if some of my money had already been settled on him – then there might have been some reason behind such a cruel action. But he was absolutely independent about money, and he would never even look at a sixpence of mine if we went on a visit. Oh, Mr Holmes! It is driving me half-mad to think of—' But the rest of the sentence was lost as the young lady sobbed quietly into her handkerchief.

When she had recovered her composure, Holmes rose from his chair, promising that he would consider the baffling facts she had put before him. 'But if I could offer you one piece of advice,' he added, as he held the lady's coat for her, 'it is that you allow Mr Horatio Darvill to vanish as completely from your memory as he vanished from his wedding-carriage.'

'Then you think that I shall not see him again?'

'I fear not. But please leave things in my hands. Now! I wish you to send me a most accurate physical description of Mr Darvill, as well as any of his letters which you feel you can spare.'

'We can at least expedite things a little in those two respects,' replied she in business-like fashion, 'for I advertised for him in last Monday's *Chronicle*.' And promptly reaching into her handbag, she produced a newspaper cutting which she gave to Holmes, together with some other sheets. 'And here, too, are four of his letters which I happen to have with me. Will they be sufficient?'

Holmes looked quickly at the letters, and nodded. 'You say you never had Mr Darvill's address?'

'Never.'

'Your step-father's place of business, please?'

'He travels for Cook and Marchant, the great Burgundy importers, of Fenchurch Street.'

'Thank you.'

After she had left Holmes sat brooding for several minutes, his fingertips still pressed together. 'An interesting case,' he observed finally. 'Did you not find it so, Watson?'

'You appeared to read a good deal which was quite invisible to me,' I confessed.

'Not invisible, Watson. Rather, let us say – unnoticed. And that in spite of my repeated attempts to impress upon you the importance of sleeves, of thumb-nails, of boot-laces, and the rest. Now, tell me, what did you immediately gather from the young woman's appearance? Describe it to me.'

Conscious of Mycroft's presence, I sought to recall my closest impressions of our recent visitor.

'Well, she had, beneath her fur, a dress of rich brown, somewhat darker than the coffee colour, with a little black plush at the neck and at the sleeves – you mentioned sleeves, Holmes? Her gloves were dove-grey in colour, and were worn through at the right forefinger. Her black boots, I was not able, from where I sat, to observe in any detail, yet I would suggest that she takes either the size four-and-a-half or five. She wore small pendant earrings, almost certainly of imitation gold, and the small handkerchief into which the poor lady sobbed so charmingly had a neat darn in the monogrammed corner. In general, she had the air of a reasonably well-to-do young woman who has not quite escaped from the slightly vulgar inheritance of a father who was – let us be honest about it, Holmes! – a plumber.'

A snort from the chair beside which Holmes had so casually thrown Miss van Allen's fur coat served to remind us that the recumbent Mycroft had now reawakened, and that perhaps my own description had, in some respect, occasioned his disapproval. But he made no spoken comment, and soon resumed his former posture.

"Pon my word, Watson,' said Holmes, 'you are coming along splendidly – is he not, Mycroft? It is true, of course, that your description misses almost everything of real importance. But the method! You have hit upon the *method*, Watson. Let us take, for example, the plush you mention on the sleeves. Now, plush is a most wonderfully helpful material for showing traces; and the double line above the wrist, where the type-writist presses against the table, was beautifully defined. As for the short-sightedness, that was mere child's play. The dent-marks of a *pince-nez* at either side of the lady's nostrils – you did not observe it? Elementary, my dear Watson! And then the boots. You really *must* practise the art of being positioned where all the evidence is clearly visible. If you wish to observe nothing at all, like brother Mycroft, then you will seek out the furthest corner of a room where even the vaguest examination of the client will be obscured by the furniture, by a fur coat, by whatever. But reverting to the lady's boots, I observed that although they were very like each other in colour and style, they were in fact *odd* boots; the one on the right foot having a slightly decorated toe-cap, and the one on the left being of a comparatively plain design.

Furthermore, the right one was fastened only at the three lower buttons out of the five; the left one only at the first, third, and fifth. Now the deduction we may reasonably draw from such evidence is that the young lady left home in an unconscionable hurry. You agree?'

'Amazing, Holmes!'

'As for the glove worn at the forefinger—'

'You would be better advised,' suddenly interposed the deeper voice of Mycroft, 'to concentrate upon the missing person.'

May it have been a flash of annoyance that showed itself in Holmes's eyes? If so, it was gone immediately. 'You are quite right, Mycroft! Come now, Watson, read to us the paragraph from *The Chronicle*.'

I held the printed slip to the light and began: 'Missing on the 14th November 188–. A gentleman named Mr Horatio Darvill: about 5 feet 8 inches in height; fairly firmly built; sallow complexion; black hair, just a little bald in the centre; bushy black side-whiskers and moustache; tinted spectacles; slight infirmity of speech. When last seen, was dressed in—'

'But I think,' interrupted Holmes, 'he may by now have changed his wedding vestments, Watson?'

'Oh, certainly, Holmes.'

There being nothing, it seemed, of further value in the newspaper description, Holmes turned his attention to the letters, passing them to me after studying them himself with minute concentration.

'Well?' he asked.

Apart from the fact that the letters had been typed, I could find in them nothing of interest, and I laid them down on the coffee-table in front of the somnolent Mycroft.

'Well?' persisted Holmes.

'I assume you refer to the fact that the letters are type-written.'

'Already you are neglecting your newly acquired knowledge of the *method*, Watson. Quite apart from the one you mention, there are three further points of immediate interest and importance. First, the letters are very short; second, apart from the vague "Leadenhall Street" superscription, there is no precise address stated at any point; third, it is not only the body of the letter which has been typed, but the signature, too. Observe here, Watson – and here! – that neat little "Horatio Darvill" typed at the bottom of each of our four exhibits. And it will not have escaped you, I think, how conclusive that last point might be?'

'Conclusive, Holmes? In what way?'

'My dear fellow, is it possible for you not to see how strongly it bears upon our present investigations?'

'*Homo circumbendibus* – that's what you are, Sherlock!' (It was Mycroft once more.) 'Do you not appreciate that your client would prefer some positive action to any further proofs of your cerebral superiority?'

It is pleasing to report here that this attempt of Mycroft to provoke the most distinguished criminologist of the century proved largely ineffectual, and Holmes permitted himself a fraternal smile as his brother slowly bestirred his frame.

'You are right, Mycroft,' he rejoined lightly. 'And I shall immediately compose two letters: one to Messrs Cook and Marchant; the other to Mr Wyndham, asking that gentleman to meet us here at six o'clock tomorrow evening.'

Already I was aware of the easy and confident demeanour with which Holmes was tackling the singular mystery which confronted us all. But for the moment my attention was diverted by a small but most curious incident.

'It is just as well, Sherlock,' said Mycroft (who appeared now to be almost fully awakened), 'that you do not propose to write three letters.'

Seldom (let me admit it) have I seen my friend so perplexed: 'A *third* letter?'

'Indeed. But such a letter could have no certain destination, since it apparently slipped your memory to ask the young lady her present address, and the letters she entrusted to you appear, as I survey them, to be lacking their outer envelopes.'

Momentarily Holmes looked less than amused by this light-hearted intervention. 'You are more observant today than I thought, Mycroft, for the evidence of eye and ear had led me to entertain the suspicion that you were sleeping soundly during my recent conversation with Miss van Allen. But as regards her address, you are right.' And even as he spoke I noted the twinkle of mischievous intelligence in his eyes. 'Yet it would not be too difficult perhaps to *deduce* the young lady's address, Mycroft? On such a foul day as this it is dangerous and ill-advised for a lady to travel the streets if she has a perfectly acceptable and comfortable alternative such as the Underground; and since it was precisely 3.14 p.m. when Miss van Allen first appeared beneath my window, I would hazard the guess that she had caught the Metropolitan-line train which passes through Baker Street at 3.12 p.m. on its journey to Hammersmith. We may consider two further clues, also. The lady's boots, ill-assorted as they were, bore little evidence of the mud and mire of our London streets; and we may infer from this that her own home is perhaps as adjacent to an Underground station as is our own. More significant, however, is the fact, as we all observed, that Miss van Allen wore a dress of linen – a fabric which, though it is long-lasting and pleasing to wear, is one which has the disadvantage of creasing most easily. Now the skirt of the dress had been most recently ironed, and the slight creases in it must have resulted from her journey – to see me. And – I put this forward as conjecture, Mycroft – probably no more than three or four stops on the Underground had been involved. If we remember, too, the "few minutes" her wedding-carriage took from her home to St Saviour's, I think, perhaps . . . perhaps . . .' Holmes drew a street-map towards him, and surveyed his chosen area with his magnification-glass.

'I shall plump,' he said directly, 'for Cowcross Street myself – that shabbily genteel little thoroughfare which links Farringdon Road with St John Street.'

'Very impressive!' said Mycroft, anticipating my own admiration. 'And would you place her on the north or the south side of that thoroughfare, Sherlock?'

But before Holmes could reply to this small pleasantry, Mrs Hudson entered with a slip of paper which she handed to Holmes. 'The young lady says she forgot to give you her address, sir, and she's written it down for you.'

Holmes glanced quickly at the address and a glint of pride gleamed in his eyes. 'The answer to your question, Mycroft, is the south side – for it is an even-numbered house, and if I remember correctly the numbering of houses in that part of London invariably begins at the east end of the street with the odd numbers on the right-hand side walking westwards.'

'And the number is perhaps in the middle or late thirties?' suggested Mycroft. 'Thirty-six, perhaps? Or more likely thirty-eight?'

Holmes himself handed over the paper to us and we read:

Miss Charlotte van Allen
38, Cowcross Street

I was daily accustomed to exhibitions of the most extraordinary deductive logic employed by Sherlock Holmes, but I had begun at this point to suspect, in his brother Mycroft, the existence of some quite paranormal mental processes. It was only some half an hour later, when Holmes himself had strolled out for tobacco, that Mycroft, observing my continued astonishment, spoke quietly in my ear.

'If you keep your lips sealed, Dr Watson, I will tell you a small secret – albeit a very simple one. The good lady's coat was thrown rather carelessly, as you noticed, over the back of a chair; and on the inside of the lining was sewn a tape with her name and address clearly printed on it. Alas, however, my eyes are now not so keen as they were in my youth, and sixes and eights, as you know, are readily susceptible of confusion.'

I have never been accused, I trust, of undue levity, but I could not help laughing heartily at this coup on Mycroft's part, and I assured him that his brother should never hear the truth of it from me.

'Sherlock?' said Mycroft, raising his mighty eyebrows. 'He saw through my little joke immediately.'

*

It was not until past six o'clock the following evening that I returned to Baker Street after (it is not an irrelevant matter) a day of deep interest at St Thomas's Hospital.

'Well, have you solved the mystery yet?' I asked, as I entered the sitting room.

Holmes I found curled up in his armchair, smoking his oily clay pipe, and discussing medieval madrigals with Mycroft.

'Yes, Watson, I believe—'

But hardly were the words from his mouth when we heard a heavy footfall in the passage and a sharp rap on the door.

'This will be the girl's step-father,' said Holmes. 'He has written to say he would be here at a quarter after six. Come in!'

The man who entered was a sturdy, middle-sized fellow, about thirty years of age, clean-shaven, sallow-skinned, with a pair of most penetrating eyes. He placed his shiny top-hat on the sideboard, and with an insinuating bow sidled down into the nearest chair.

'I am assuming,' said Holmes, 'that you are Mr James Wyndham and' (holding up a type-written sheet) 'that this is the letter you wrote to me?'

'I am that person, sir, and the letter is mine. It was against my expressed wish, as you may know, that Miss van Allen contacted you in this matter. But she is an excitable young lady, and my wife and I will be happy to forgive her for such an impulsive action. Yet I must ask you to have nothing more to do with what is, unfortunately, a not uncommon misfortune. It is clear what took place, and I think it highly unlikely, sir, that even you will find so much as a single trace of Mr Darvill.'

'On the contrary,' replied Holmes quietly, 'I have reason to believe that I have already discovered the whereabouts of that gentleman.'

Mr Wyndham gave a violent start, and dropped his gloves. 'I am delighted to hear it,' he said in a strained voice.

'It is a most curious fact,' continued Holmes, 'that a type-writer has just as much individuality as does handwriting. Even when completely new, no two machines are exactly alike; and as they get older, some characters wear on this side and some on that. Now in this letter of yours, Mr Wyndham, you will note that in every instance there is some slight slurring in the eye of the "e"; and a most easily detectable defect in the tail of the "t".'

'All our office correspondence,' interrupted our visitor, 'is typed on the same machine, and I can fully understand why it has become a little worn.'

'But I have four other letters here,' resumed Holmes, in a slow and menacing tone, 'which purport to come from Mr Horatio Darvill. And in each of these, also, the "e"s are slurred, and the "t"s un-tailed.'

Mr Wyndham was out of his chair instantly and had snatched up his hat. 'I can waste no more of my valuable time with such trivialities, Mr Holmes. If you can catch the man who so shamefully treated Miss van Allen, then catch him! I wish you well – and ask you to let me know the outcome. But I have no interest whatsoever in your fantastical notions.'

Already, however, Holmes had stepped across the room and turned the key in the door. 'Certainly I will tell you how I caught Mr Darvill, if you will but resume your chair.'

'What?' shouted Wyndham, his face white, his small eyes darting about him like those of a rat in a trap. Yet finally he sat down and glared aggressively around, as Holmes continued his analysis.

'It was as selfish and as heartless a trick as ever I encountered. The man married a woman much older than himself, largely for her money. In addition, he enjoyed the interest on the not inconsiderable sum of the step-daughter's money, for as long as that daughter lived with them. The loss of such extra monies would have made a significant difference to the lifestyle adopted by the newly married pair. Now the daughter herself was an amiable, warm-hearted girl, and was possessed of considerable physical attractions; and with the added advantage of a personal income, it became clear that under normal circumstances she would not remain single for very long. So he – the man of whom I speak – decided to deny her the company and friendship of her contemporaries by keeping her at home. But she – and who shall blame her? – grew restive under such an unnatural regimen, and firmly announced her intention to attend a local ball. So what did her step-father do? With the connivance of his wife, he conceived a cowardly plan. He disguised himself cleverly: he covered those sharp eyes with dully tinted spectacles; he masked that clean-shaven face with bushy side-whiskers; he sank that clear voice of his into the strained whisper of one suffering from the quinsy. And then, feeling himself doubly secure because of the young lady's short sight, he appeared *himself* at the ball, in the guise of one Horatio Darvill, and there he wooed the fair Miss van Allen for his own – thereafter taking the further precaution of always arranging his assignations by candlelight.'

(I heard a deep groan which at the time I assumed to have come from our visitor, but which, upon reflection, I am inclined to think originated from Mycroft's corner.)

'Miss van Allen had fallen for her new beau; and no suspicion of deception ever entered her pretty head. She was flattered by the attention she was receiving, and the effect was heightened by the admiration of her mother for the man. An "engagement" was agreed, and the deception perpetuated. But the pretended journeys abroad were becoming more difficult to sustain, and things had to be brought to a head quickly, although in such a *dramatic* way as to leave a permanent impression upon the young girl's mind. Hence the vows of fidelity sworn on the Testaments; hence the dark hints repeated on the very morning of the proposed marriage that something sinister might be afoot. James Wyndham, you see, wished his step-daughter to be so morally bound to her fictitious suitor that for a decade, at least, she would sit and wilt in Cowcross Street, and continue paying her regular interest directly into the account of her guardian: the same blackguard of a guardian who had brought her to the doors of St Saviour's and then, himself, conveniently disappeared by the age-old ruse of stepping in at one side of a four-wheeler – and out at the other.'

Rising to his feet, Wyndham fought hard to control his outrage. 'I wish you to know that it is you, sir, who is violating the law of this land – and not me! As long as you keep that door locked, and thereby hold me in this room against my will, you lay yourself open—'

'The law,' interrupted Holmes, suddenly unlocking and throwing open the door, 'may not for the moment be empowered to touch you. Yet never, surely, was there a man who deserved punishment more. In fact . . . since my hunting-crop is close at hand—' Holmes took two swift strides across the room; but it was too late. We heard a wild clatter of steps down the stairs as Wyndham departed, and then had the satisfaction of watching him flee pell-mell down Baker Street.

'That cold-blooded scoundrel will end on the gallows, mark my words!' growled Holmes.

'Even now, though, I cannot follow all the steps in your reasoning, Holmes,' I remarked.

'It is this way,' replied Holmes. 'The only person who profited financially from the vanishing-trick – was the step-father. Then, the fact that the two men, Wyndham and Darvill, were never actually seen *together*, was most suggestive. As were the tinted spectacles, the husky voice, the bushy whiskers – all of these latter, Watson, hinting strongly at disguise. Again, the type-written signature betokened one thing only – that the man's handwriting was so familiar to Miss van Allen that she might easily recognize even a small sample of it. Isolated facts? Yes! But all of them leading to the same inevitable conclusion – as even my slumbering sibling might agree?'

But there was no sound from the Mycroft corner.

'You were able to verify your conclusion?' I asked.

Holmes nodded briskly. 'We know the firm for which Wyndham worked, and we had a full description of Darvill. I therefore eliminated from that description everything which could be the result of deliberate disguise—'

'Which means that you have *not* verified your conclusion!' Mycroft's sudden interjection caused us both to turn sharply towards him.

'There will always,' rejoined Holmes, 'be a need and a place for informed conjecture—'

'*Inspired* conjecture, Holmes,' I interposed.

'Phooey!' snorted Mycroft. 'You are talking of nothing but wild *guesswork*, Sherlock. And it is my opinion that in this case your guesswork is grotesquely askew.'

I can only report that never have I seen Holmes so taken aback; and he sat in silence as Mycroft raised his bulk from the chair and now stood beside the fireplace.

'Your deductive logic needs no plaudits from me, Sherlock, and like Dr Watson I admire your desperate hypothesis. But unless there is some firm evidence which you have thus far concealed from us . . . ?'

Holmes did not break his silence.

'Well,' stated Mycroft, 'I will indulge in a little guesswork of my own, and tell you that the gentleman who just stormed out of this room is as innocent as Watson here!'

'He certainly did not *act* like an innocent man,' I protested, looking in vain to Holmes for some support, as Mycroft continued.

'The reasons you adduce for your suspicions are perfectly sound in most respects, and yet – I must speak with honesty, Sherlock! – I found myself sorely disappointed with your reading – or rather complete misreading – of the case. You are, I believe, wholly correct in your central thesis that there is no such person as Horatio Darvill.' (How the blood was tingling in my veins as Mycroft spoke these words!) 'But when the unfortunate Mr Wyndham, who has just rushed one way up Baker Street, rushes back down it the other with a writ for defamation of character – as I fear he will! – then

114

you will be compelled to think, to analyse, and to act, with a little more care and circumspection.'

Holmes leaned forward, the sensitive nostrils of that aquiline nose a little distended. But still he made no comment.

'For example, Sherlock, two specific pieces of information vouchsafed to us by the attractive Miss van Allen herself have been strongly discounted, if not wholly ignored, in your analysis.' (I noticed Holmes's eyebrows rising quizzically.) 'First, the fact that Mr Wyndham was older than Miss van Allen *only by some five years*. Second, the fact that Miss van Allen is so competent and speedy a performer on the typewriter that she works, on a free-lance basis, for several firms in the vicinity of her home, including Messrs Cook and Marchant. Furthermore, you make the astonishing claim that Miss van Allen was totally deceived by the disguise of Mr Darvill. Indeed, you would have her not only blind, but semi-senile into the bargain! Now it is perfectly true that the lady's eyesight is far from perfect – *glaucopia Athenica*, would you not diagnose, Dr Watson? – but it is quite ludicrous to believe that she would fail to recognize the person with whom she was living. And it is wholly dishonest of you to assert that the assignations were always held by candlelight, since on at least two occasions, the morning after the first meeting – the *morning*, Sherlock! – and the morning of the planned wedding ceremony, Miss van Allen had ample opportunity of studying the physical features of Darvill in the broadest of daylight.'

'You seem to me to be taking an unconscionably long time in putting forward your own hypothesis,' snapped Holmes, somewhat testily.

'You are right,' admitted the other. 'Let me beat about the

bush no longer! You have never felt emotion akin to love for any woman, Sherlock – not even for the Adler woman – and you are therefore deprived of the advantages of those who like myself are able to understand both the workings of the male and also the female mind. Five years her superior in age – her step-father; *only five years.* Now one of the sadnesses of womankind is their tendency to age more quickly and less gracefully than men; and one of the truths about mankind in general is that if you put one of each sex, of roughly similar age, in reasonable proximity ... And if one of them is the fair Miss van Allen – then you are inviting a packet of trouble. Yet such is what took place in the Wyndham ménage. Mrs Wyndham was seventeen years older than her young husband; and perhaps as time went by some signs and tokens of this disproportionate difference in their ages began to manifest themselves. At the same time, it may be assumed that Wyndham himself could not help being attracted – however much at first he sought to resist the temptation – by the very winsome and vivacious young girl who was his step-daughter. It would almost certainly have been Wyndham himself who introduced Miss van Allen to the part-time duties she undertook for Cook and Marchant – where the two of them were frequently thrown together, away from the restraints of wife and home, and with a result which it is not at all difficult to guess. Certain it is, in my own view, that Wyndham sought to transfer his affections from the mother to the daughter; and in due course it was the daughter who decided that whatever her own affections might be in the matter she must in all honour leave her mother and step-father. Hence the great anxiety to get out to dances and parties and the like – activities which Wyndham objected to for the obvious reason that he wished to have Miss van Allen as close by himself for as long as he possibly could. Now you, Sherlock, assume that this objection arose as a result of the interest accruing from the New Zealand securities – and you are *guessing*, are you not? Is it not just possible that Wyndham has money of his own – find out, brother! – and that what he craves for is not some petty addition to his wealth, but the love of a young woman with whom he has fallen rather hopelessly in love? You see, she took *him* in, just as she took *you* in, Sherlock – for you swallowed everything that calculating little soul reported.'

'Really, this is outrageous!' I objected – but Holmes held up his hand, and bid me hear his brother out.

'What is clear, is that at some point when Wyndham was in France – and why did you not verify those dates spent abroad? I am sure Cook and Marchant would have provided them just as quickly as it furnished the wretched man's description. But as I was saying, with Wyndham in France, mother and daughter found themselves in a little *tête-à-tête* one evening, during the course of which a whole basketful of dirty linen was laid bare, with the daughter bitterly disillusioned about the behaviour of her step-father, and the mother hurt and angry about her husband's infidelity. So, together, the pair of them devised a plan. Now, we both agree on one thing at least, Sherlock! There appears to be no evidence whatsoever for the independent existence of Horatio Darvill except for what we have heard from Miss van Allen's lips. Rightly, you drew our attention to the fact that the two men were never seen together. But, alas, having appreciated the *importance* of that clue, you completely misconceived its *significance*. *You* decided that there is no Darvill – because he

is Wyndham. *I* have to tell you that there is no Darvill –
*because he is the pure fabrication of the minds of Mrs Wyndham and
her daughter.*'

Holmes was staring with some consternation at a pattern
in the carpet, as Mycroft rounded off his extravagant and
completely baseless conjectures.

'Letters were written – and incidentally I myself would
have been far more cautious about those "e"s and "t"s: twin
faults, as it happens, of my very own machine! But, as I say,
letters were written – *but by Miss van Allen herself*; a wedding
was arranged; a story concocted of a non-existent carriage
into which there climbed a non-existent groom – and that
was the end of the charade. Now, it was you, Sherlock, who
rightly asked the key question: *cui bono*? And you concluded
that the real beneficiary was Wyndham. But exactly the
contrary is the case! It was the mother and daughter who
intended to be the beneficiaries, for they hoped to rid
themselves of the rather wearisome Mr Wyndham – but not
before he had been compelled, by moral and social pressures,
to make some handsome money-settlement upon the pair of
them – especially perhaps upon the young girl who, as Dr
Watson here points out, could well have done with some
decent earrings and a new handkerchief. And the *social*
pressure I mention, Sherlock, was designed – carefully and
cleverly designed – to come from *you*. A cock-and-bull story
is told to you by some wide-eyed young thing, a story so
bestrewn with clues at almost every point that even Lestrade
– given a week or two! – would probably have come up with
a diagnosis identical with your own. And why do you think
she came to you, and not to Lestrade, say? Because "Mr
Sherlock Holmes is the greatest investigator the world has

ever known" – and his judgements are second only to the Almighty's in their infallibility. For if you, Sherlock, believed Wyndham to be guilty – then Wyndham *was* guilty in the eyes of the whole world – the whole world except for one, that is.'

'Except for two,' I added quietly.

Mycroft Holmes turned his full attention towards me for the first time, as though I had virtually been excluded from his previous audience. But I allowed him no opportunity of seeking the meaning of my words, as I addressed him forthwith.

'I asked Holmes a question when he presented his own analysis, sir. I will ask you the same: have you in any way verified your hypothesis? And if so, how?'

'The answer, Dr Watson, to the first part of your question is, in large measure, "yes". Mr Wyndham, in fact, has quite enough money to be in no way embarrassed by the withdrawal of Miss van Allen's comparatively minor contribution. As for the second part . . .' Mycroft hesitated awhile. 'I am not sure what my brother has told you of the various offices I hold under the British Crown—'

It was Holmes who intervened – and impatiently so. 'Yes, yes, Mycroft! Let us all concede immediately that the, shall we say, "unofficial" sources to which you are privy have completely invalidated my own reconstruction of the case. So be it! Yet I would wish, if you allow, to make one or two observations upon your own rather fanciful interpretation of events? It is, of course, with full justice that you accuse me of having no first-hand knowledge of what are called "the matters of the heart". Furthermore, you rightly draw attention to the difficulties Mr Wyndham would have experienced in deceiving his step-daughter. Yet how you under-rate the power of disguise! And how, incidentally, you *over*-rate the intelligence of Lestrade! Even Dr Watson, I would suggest, has a brain considerably superior—'

For not a second longer could I restrain myself. 'Gentlemen!' I cried. 'You are both – *both* of you! – most tragically wrong.'

The two brothers stared at me as though I had taken leave of my senses.

'I think you should seek to explain yourself, Watson,' said Holmes sharply.

'A man,' I began, 'was proposing to go to Scotland for a fortnight with his newly married wife, and he had drawn out one hundred pounds in cash – no less! – from the Oxford Street branch of the Royal National Bank on the eve of his wedding. The man, however, was abducted after entering a four-wheeler on the very morning of his wedding-day, was brutally assaulted, and then robbed of all his money and personal effects – thereafter being dumped, virtually for dead, in a deserted alley in Stepney. Quite by chance he was discovered later that same evening, and taken to the White-chapel Hospital. But it was only after several days that the man slowly began to recover his senses, and some patches of his memory – and also, gentlemen, his *voice*. For, you see, it was partly because the man was suffering so badly from what we medical men term suppurative tonsilitis – the quinsy, as it is commonly known – that he was transferred to St Thomas's where, as you know, Holmes, I am at present engaged in some research on that very subject, and where my own professional opinion was sought only this morning. Whilst reading through the man's hospital notes, I could see that the only clue to his identity was a tag on an item of his underclothing carrying the initials "H. D.". You can imagine my excitement—'

'Humphry Davey, perhaps,' muttered Mycroft flippantly.

'Oh no!' I replied, with a smile. 'I persisted patiently with the poor man, and finally he was able to communicate to me the name of his bank. After that, if I may say so, Holmes, it was almost child's play to verify *my* hypothesis. I visited the bank, where I learned about the withdrawal of money for the honeymoon, and the manager himself accompanied me back to St Thomas's where he was able to view the patient and to provide quite unequivocal proof as to his identity. I have to inform you, therefore, that not only does Mr Horatio Darvill exist, gentlemen, he is at this precise moment lying in a private ward on the second floor of St Thomas's Hospital!'

For some little while a silence fell upon the room. Then I saw Holmes, who these last few minutes had been standing by the window, give a little start. 'Oh, no!' he groaned. And looking over his shoulder I saw, dimly beneath the fog-beshrouded lamplight, an animated Mr Wyndham talking to a legal-looking gentleman who stood beside him.

Snatching up his cape, Holmes made hurriedly for the door. 'Please tell Mr Wyndham, if you will, Watson, that I have already written a letter to him containing a complete recantation of my earlier charges, and offering him my profound apologies. For the present, I am leaving – by the back door.'

He was gone. And when, a minute later, Mrs Hudson announced that two angry-looking gentlemen had called asking to see Mr Holmes, I noticed Mycroft seemingly asleep once more in his corner armchair, a monograph on polyphonic plainchant open on his knee, and a smile of vague amusement on his large, intelligent face.

'Show the gentlemen in, please, Mrs Hudson!' I said – in such peremptory fashion that for a moment or two that good lady stared at me, almost as if she had mistaken my voice for that of Sherlock Holmes himself.